GH

Dancing with the Dead

GHOSTHUNTERS

Dancing with the Dead

Anthony Masters

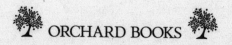

ORCHARD BOOKS

ORCHARD BOOKS
96 Leonard Street, London EC2A 4RH
Orchard Books Australia
14 Mars Road, Lane Cove, NSW 2066
ISBN 1 86039 818 9
First published as a paperback original in Great Britain1998
Text © Anthony Masters 1998
A CIP catalogue record for this book is available
from the British Library.
Printed and bound in Great Britain

CHAPTER ONE

'I'd rather fish,' said Terry. 'It's windy out there.'
He gazed out at the grey-green waves whipped up
by the strengthening breeze. 'Besides – I don't
much like being on the sea nowadays.'

'You said you could swim.' David was impatient.
'And you've been sailing *Sunrise* for years, haven't
you?'

'Oh yes, I can swim all right. That's not the
problem.' Terry sounded uneasy, as if he was up
against questions he couldn't answer. 'I've just gone
off dinghies, that's all. I prefer fishing.'

'What's the problem then?' Jenny was already
exasperated with her sulky cousin, and she and
David had only been in Swinton a couple of days.

'None of your business,' Terry muttered, casting
his line and avoiding the twins' irritated gaze. 'Now
why don't you push off and leave me in peace?' He
paused and then added, 'And if you *are* going to
take *Sunrise* out, don't go near that red marker

5

buoy. It's dangerous out there.'

David was about to ask Terry what he meant when he saw the now familiar shut-in look on his cousin's face. He decided against probing any further because he knew he wouldn't get anywhere. But somehow he and Jenny had to find out what was really bothering Terry.

After they had been sailing *Sunrise* for half an hour the wind freshened still further, but the twins weren't bothered. They were already experienced sailors, often taking out the family dinghy on the Thames near where they lived in East London. They had also just finished a sailing course in Devon while on holiday with their parents, so they were able to handle *Sunrise* with ease.

Jenny took the helm and mainsail while David concentrated on the jib. Soon she took the dinghy about, the spray sheeting over *Sunrise*'s bows, soaking their life-jackets, glistening silver in the sparkling sunlight.

Suddenly they heard a bell chiming and the spray seemed to turn freezing cold. Both David and Jenny went rigid. Where could the sound be coming from?

Glancing back, David saw Terry standing up on the old jetty, rigidly gazing out to sea, as if he had heard the chiming too. Then he began to wave urgently at them. Was he trying to tell them something? David caught sight of the red marker buoy bobbing to starboard. The twins hadn't bothered to take any notice of Terry's advice and David glanced at his sister apprehensively.

'What was that?' she yelled.

'Sounded like a bell.'

The hollow booming came again, but the twins didn't have time to dwell on the strange sound as the wind suddenly sent *Sunrise* hurtling across the bay. It was incredibly exhilarating. Long gusts filled the sail and they could really feel her speed as the dinghy scudded along, her wake frothing behind.

As *Sunrise* continued to head out to sea David remembered why Mum had wanted them to visit her sister's family.

Betty and Trevor Todd, the twins' aunt and uncle, owned the Fisherman's Rest, a fourteenth-century pub that stood on the quayside at Swinton, a small town on the Suffolk coast. Terry was their only son. The Todds employed an old couple, Charlie and Rose Hamilton, to help them run the Fisherman's Rest, and Terry was devoted to both of them. Then, last summer, when Terry was only just thirteen, Rose Hamilton had drowned.

David frowned, trying to remember exactly

what Mum had said. Slowly her words returned to him.

'No one knows what happened that night. She came from a fishing family but she'd never learnt to swim and she was afraid of the sea, so it's all a mystery. Anyway, she was found drowned and I know Terry grieved as much as Charlie did. Now they've both got so withdrawn. You can understand it in an old man, but not in a young boy like Terry. It must be because our own parents died so long ago. The Hamiltons were the grandparents he never had. Anyway, I don't know what's to be done about him and neither do Betty and Trevor. I'd be so grateful if you could go down for a few days and try and get Terry out of his shell. Do a bit of sailing with him. He won't see any friends and just sits on the jetty and fishes and mopes.'

'Ready about!' yelled Jenny, cutting into her twin's thoughts. They changed to the opposite bow, ducking under the boom and leaning out over the side as *Sunrise* turned on her next tack, heading back to the shore again.

'What are we going to do about Terry?' yelled David once the dinghy was set on course again. 'I'm sure he's holding something back.'

'What *can* we do about him? He's locked into himself,' Jenny shouted. 'We've tried, haven't we?

And we're not getting anywhere.'

'I reckon there's more to it than Rose Hamilton's death.'

'What do you mean?' Jenny was surprised. 'That's enough, isn't it?'

'When I look at him, he seems to be always watching the sea. As if he's waiting for something to happen.'

As he spoke they both heard the hollow booming again and realised they had tacked back to the red marker buoy. It was almost as if *Sunrise* had found her own way. The booming was louder this time and sounded like a muffled but increasingly deafening bell. When Jenny gazed at her twin she saw he was holding his ears.

In sudden panic, Jenny let go of the tiller. She grabbed at it again but was too late; a gust of wind caught the sail, the dinghy spun round and began to capsize.

The twins were thrown out into what seemed, despite the summer heat, a bitterly cold sea. Gasping, Jenny swam round to the prow of *Sunrise* while David made for the keel. Then he saw the ruined steeple of a church shimmering under the water.

At first David thought that the shock of the capsize had made him hallucinate. He closed his eyes and opened them again, hoping the ruined steeple might have gone away, but it hadn't. Stunted, broken in several parts, cloaked in seaweed, the steeple seemed horribly close to the surface. No wonder there was a marker buoy.

'Get on the keel!' yelled Jenny.

'Hang on. Swim over here. I want to show you something.'

As Jenny splashed her way towards him, they both heard the hollow booming again, and David was sure he saw the wavering shadow vibrate below him.

'Look at that,' he said as Jenny joined him.

'I don't believe it!'

'Neither did I. But it's there right enough. Isn't it?'

Jenny nodded. They both continued to gaze down and could clearly see the weed-hung steeple.

'Why didn't Terry tell us?' she spluttered.

'He did. He told us not to go near the red marker buoy because it was dangerous. What more could he have said?'

'You don't sail over a church steeple every day of the week.'

'We're not sailing! We've capsized. It's almost as if *Sunrise* was pulled back to the steeple.'

'Let's get her upright and stop going on about

it,' yelled Jenny.

But despite the twins' best efforts the dinghy, which should have righted itself in the capsize drill, seemed reluctant to co-operate. She was as heavy as lead.

'We're drifting back to the harbour. We've got to get her up or Terry will think we're idiots,' David shouted.

'OK,' wheezed Jenny, who was beginning to feel so cold she could hardly move. 'Let's go through the capsize drill again.' Why *was* the water so piercingly cold over the drowned church, she wondered.

'Hurry up,' yelled David. 'The tide's pushing us right in. We're going to look like absolute—'

He stopped in mid-sentence as Jenny let out a cry of panic.

Something was wrapped around her foot. Could it be one of the ropes that controlled the mainsail or the jib? Whatever it was, the more she struggled the more she was held fast.

'I'm tangled up,' she shouted. 'Something in the rigging.'

'Kick,' her twin advised her.

'That makes it worse.'

'OK. I'm coming.' David swam round the stern of *Sunrise*, wincing at the cold, noticing that despite

11

her life-jacket Jenny's shoulders were under water and only her head was breaking the surface.

'Something's pulling me down,' she screamed.

David was beside her now, grabbing at her shoulders, but a large wave swamped her, from which she emerged choking. Trying to control his panic, he dived down to see what was trapping his sister.

David opened his eyes under the cloudy surface and his heart began to pound. Something that looked like a silky sheet was tangled around Jenny's legs. The rest of it floated down to the broken spire of the drowned church.

He grabbed at the silky stuff, but it was tight and his hands couldn't get any purchase as he dragged at the slippery, slimy substance.

When David was forced to break surface again he could see that Jenny was even lower in the water. Desperately he turned towards the jetty and saw that Terry was still standing there, watching them closely.

'Help!' yelled David as he and Jenny dipped up and down in the troughs of the waves. 'We need help!'

As he rose again David saw long blond hair on a wave as Terry swam powerfully towards the capsized dinghy, his bulk no longer clumsy but ideally built for cleaving through the swell.

Just as Jenny's nose began to submerge, he was beside them. 'What's happening?' he asked, hardly gasping at all.

'This stuff. It's round her legs.'

Terry pulled a penknife out of his jeans pocket and dived. A few seconds later Jenny swam free, fighting for breath and spluttering. Then Terry surfaced, his face grey with fear.

'I *told* you not to sail near the buoy.' Terry hung on to the upturned *Sunrise*, looking furious, while Jenny and David grabbed her keel.

'What *was* that stuff?' Jenny was shivering violently. 'It was like silk.'

'Maybe it was weed that surged up on some kind of freak current,' suggested Terry.

Jenny nodded, just glad to be alive, but David noticed that their cousin was gazing down at the sea with a kind of fearful anger.

'You saved my life,' said Jenny. 'I'm so grateful.'

'Me too,' said David, feeling ashamed. 'I couldn't shift the weed – or whatever it was.'

Terry suddenly jerked into action. 'Let's get *Sunrise* the right way up. And next time – don't *ever* go near that buoy.'

Jenny wanted to confide in him about what they had seen, but something in Terry's pale, tense face held her back.

By the time they had righted *Sunrise* and baled her out, Jenny and David were exhausted and Terry helmed the dinghy back to the harbour, proving himself to be a highly competent sailor.

'There are some unpredictable currents out there,' he said suddenly, as if more explanation was needed. 'You need to be careful.'

'We messed that up,' said Jenny, her lips blue with cold. 'We're sorry.'

'It was just bad luck,' Terry replied with unexpected generosity, as if he wanted to forget all about the incident as quickly as he could. 'You're pretty good sailors. Both of you.'

'Then why not come out with us?' asked David, seizing his opportunity.

Terry shook his head. 'No way,' he said. 'I don't want to chance it again.' Then he looked confused and embarrassed, as if he wished he hadn't spoken.

Chance what again, wondered the twins.

As they sailed back, Jenny gazed out at the shoreline. The jetty belonged to the pub and was in disrepair, but the harbour, a little further along the shore, was in good working order. The fishing fleet was out at sea, but there were other craft bobbing up and down on their moorings.

Swinton was a mixture of ancient cottages and a few modern buildings, including an amusement arcade, a large fish and chip shop and a small and rather run-down-looking boating lake. Not many visitors came, for there was nothing to do but sail or swim, and that didn't seem to attract them. It was strange, thought Jenny. The harbour was beautiful and the beaches had loads of sand at low tide.

As *Sunrise* sped towards the jetty, Jenny once again wondered if they should tell Terry about the bell's hollow booming under the sea and once again she decided against it. There was something about her cousin's anxiety that needed careful handling if she and David were ever going to learn the truth.

CHAPTER TWO

Terry must have been stocky and good-looking once, with a mane of blond hair that tumbled over his wide shoulders, but now he was vast. His belly hung over his jeans, and although his face was deeply tanned it was round and podgy.

The twins had to admit that Aunty Betty didn't exactly help. High tea in the Todd family was an event not to be missed, and even when Uncle Trevor and Charlie Hamilton had departed to prepare the pub for evening opening, Aunty Betty still presided over a feast set out on a scrubbed pine table in the big kitchen that served as the family living room.

Betty was a square-faced, good-humoured woman with the same silky blonde hair as her son, except that she wore it piled up on top of her head.

No wonder Terry's so fat, thought Jenny as she took an enormous piece of pork pie, adding a generous dollop of the potato salad that Aunty

Betty had just brought in, almost as an afterthought.

Encouraged by the fact that the Todds hadn't been as upset about the capsize as his parents would have been, David was now determined to raise the subject of what they had seen and heard by the red marker buoy.

After some hesitation, he blurted out self-consciously, 'We heard this bell – at least I think it was a bell – and then we saw the spire of a church – under the water.' David finished in a rush, his words tumbling over each other and then faltering as he glanced across at Terry, whose face had once again gone grey under his tan, one hand shaking so much that he spilt potato salad on the table.

Aunty Betty quickly intervened, trying to sound calm and normal, as if drowned church spires and hollow bells were all part of everyday life in Swinton. But both the twins had noticed that for a moment she, too, had looked decidedly uneasy.

'I don't know about a bell,' she said. 'But the fishermen say some of the spire's still there. They really built well in those days, didn't they? I mean, for a building to survive the sea for so long—'

'How did it happen?' David interrupted. 'How did the village get drowned?' The atmosphere had changed from being happily relaxed to brightly uneasy.

Betty paused and then hurried on. 'The land was always low lying and the sea had been encroaching for some time. Then, in 1896, a tidal wave drowned the church and its graveyard, as well as the church hall and some cottages.' She paused again. 'At most tides you can get to some of the ruins, but not the church. It's too far out,' she added warningly.

'But what about the bell?' asked Jenny curiously. 'Surely that wouldn't have survived under all that pressure? If part of the spire is missing, then wouldn't the bell have been carried away?'

'Of course,' Betty agreed. 'You must have been mistaken.'

There was a long silence during which Terry glanced at his mother and then back to his plate again. 'I've never heard a bell,' he said sourly.

'What you heard was the automatic warning on the buoy by the rocks. That makes a hollow booming,' said Aunty Betty briskly.

'Everything's distorted under water,' added Terry. 'It's strange how it can fool you.'

Jenny suddenly remembered the feel of the silky stuff round her feet, gripping so tightly that she knew she stood no chance against it, dragging her down to the spire and to whatever lay on the sea bed.

'Are you all right, love?' asked Aunty Betty. 'You look as if you've seen a ghost.'

After tea, Terry sat down heavily in front of the TV and began to watch a succession of soap operas. Excluded, Jenny and David wandered out into the passageway that connected the kitchen with the bar of the pub and also led to the back door.

'Let's go down to the beach,' David said, yawning. 'The tide's going out. Maybe we'll see the ruins.'

'OK,' said Jenny. Anything was better than watching soap operas with Terry.

As the twins walked down the dark corridor they noticed a large picture in a black frame. Behind the dusty glass was a painting of a huge tidal wave heading towards a church with a high spire.

The twins exchanged glances, and moved closer, trying to decipher the faded lettering.

DANCING WITH THE DEAD –
THE SWINTON LEGEND

On August 15th 1896, St Stephen's and its grave-yard, together with the church hall and twelve cottages, were overwhelmed by a tidal wave. The sea had been eroding the coastline for centuries. At the time of the disaster, a dance was being held in the church hall.

Each year, on the anniversary of the tragedy, the drowned are reputed to return to the streets of Swinton to dance with the living. If anyone links hands with the drowned, they will be taken under the sea.

'It's the anniversary tomorrow,' said a gravelly voice.

Jenny and David turned round, hearts pounding, to see Charlie Hamilton standing behind them, a crate of empty beer bottles in his arms. He put it down and gazed at the twins intently through his huge pebble-lensed glasses.

Charlie was in his early seventies and was tall, well over six foot. Once he must have been power-fully built, but now he was so thin that he looked like a dry and brittle stick-man with a tweed jacket that seemed too big for him, a tightly knotted tie and old corduroy trousers. He was completely bald except for two tufts of hair just over his ears.

'The dead will come dancing.'

'It was a terrible tragedy,' said Jenny, trying not to be intimidated by him.

'I lost my sister to them – to the drowned. The Swinton Drowned. They came for my Rose and left me on my own. I never married. Never had kiddies. Rose was all I had.'

Charlie was deeply moved, clearly feeling his loss as keenly as if it had happened yesterday rather than last year.

Charlie picked up his crate of empty bottles. 'They wouldn't have that picture in the snug where it's always been. Not after Rose. So it's out here now. But it don't matter. Swinton folk don't need to be reminded about dancing with the dead. You keep inside tomorrow night. It's the lowest tide of the year and they'll be coming out of their shrouds. I just wish they'd take me so I could be with my Rose again.'

Shrouds? David gazed at Jenny, the fear creeping inside him with a cold chill. The silky stuff that had tried to drag Jenny down. Could *that* have been a shroud? He saw that she was staring back at him, her eyes full of anxiety, the memory of the freezing water and the silky substance making her shiver. Of course it must have been weed, but how could the stuff have been so strong? How could it leap up at her like that from the depths? Terry's theory about currents seemed feeble. Not just feeble. Downright impossible.

Jenny remembered the water filling her mouth. If it hadn't been for Terry she could have joined the drowned of Swinton. She gazed up at the old man's face, trying to see his eyes behind the thick glasses.

Charlie Hamilton abruptly left the twins, hurrying on down the passageway. He opened a battered door that led to the cellar and they heard his footsteps clattering down the stairs.

'I wonder if his sister was as short-sighted as he is?' David whispered. 'Maybe she just walked into the sea by mistake.'

'Don't be horrible.'

'What other reason could there have been?' he demanded, but Jenny knew her twin was as afraid as she was.

Again the bar door opened and this time Uncle Trevor came through. He immediately looked concerned when he saw David and Jenny's eyes riveted on the legend.

'I suppose Charlie's been going on about the Swinton Drowned,' he said irritably. Then he grinned. Trevor was a big man but unlike Terry hadn't got so fat. He had broad shoulders, a tough, friendly face and huge arms with rippling muscles. Apart from owning the pub, he was also a member of the lifeboat crew. 'Personally, I don't accept a word of it and never will.' He looked at them strangely and Jenny had the impression he had steeled himself against believing in the legend and that his determination was strong.

'He was talking about dancing with the dead,' David blurted out.

'He would, wouldn't he? It's his sister Rose – she drowned and it turned him. Great strapping man he was. Like me only better built. Used to run the village shop with Rose before they both came to work for me. Since her death he's gone to pieces. It's all a terrible tragedy but I don't want him frightening you.'

'He wasn't,' said Jenny loyally. 'He just wanted to talk, that's all.'

'On his favourite subject.'

'I think he *needed* to talk about it,' David suggested. 'What happened to the shop?'

'They went bust. Charlie and Rose couldn't compete with the supermarket.'

'What was Rose like?' asked Jenny curiously.

Trevor Todd paused and his expression softened. 'She was a wonderful lady. Warm and kind and really good. She was like a mother to me and Betty, and a grandmother to Terry. That's why he's been so down. We all miss Rose dreadfully, but Charlie and Terry the most. Her death took something out of them, something precious. As you can see. But don't let Charlie scare you with his morbid ways.'

'He says the anniversary's tomorrow,' said David hesitantly.

'So what? I just told you I don't believe all that stuff. Betty doesn't either, and neither should you.'

'Does Terry?'

Trevor's face clouded. 'He's not himself. He used to be so outgoing – and he loved sailing like you do. My boy's gone downhill, like Charlie.' Trevor turned away from them as the twins saw tears come to his eyes, but when he swung back he had blinked them away. 'That's why I'm glad – so glad – you two have come. I gather Terry swam out to give you a hand when you capsized this afternoon.'

'He was brilliant,' said David admiringly. 'Terrific swimmer.'

'Yes, he is. But since Rose drowned he won't go anywhere near the sea. In fact this must be the first time he's been in. Sometimes I think I should get rid of Charlie. I'm sure he has a bad influence on Terry, but I don't really see how – except they're both in mourning for her. Fair enough – Charlie's an old man and Rose was all he had. But Terry, he's only thirteen and a strong, healthy boy. Or he was. Look at the weight he's putting on. All that comfort food.' Uncle Trevor checked himself, conscious that he was running on. 'If you can get him back on *Sunrise*, I'd be grateful.'

He hurried back to the bar, leaving the twins

wondering if they should have mentioned the hollow booming bell again – the drowned bell as David thought of it. In the end, Jenny decided that it was a good thing they hadn't. Uncle Trevor had enough on his mind.

CHAPTER THREE

The wind had dropped and the night was warm as Jenny and David strolled along the shingle beach.

'The tide's still going out,' said David, smelling mud and weed.

'How could Rose have drowned if she was afraid of the sea?' wondered Jenny.

'A freak wave?'

'There seem to have been a lot of freak waves in Swinton,' she replied despondently.

The twins stood on the edge of the pebbles. In the shadowy and pallid light of a large, waxy full moon they could see a vast expanse of flat sandy mud with the sea sighing and lapping on the horizon.

'The stars are reflected in the water,' said Jenny quietly. 'Aren't they beautiful?'

'They don't match.' David's voice was bleak.

'*What?*'

'They don't match. Look for yourself. They

aren't reflections. They're lights.'

'You can't have lights under the sea.'

'You can at Swinton,' said David fearfully.

Then they heard the music.

The sound had a strangely intoxicating rhythm, and although they could barely make out the melody, David and Jenny could feel it swirling in their heads and down into their feet. A drum beat, a fiddle played, an accordion wailed – together they made the most exciting sound either of the twins had ever heard. Slowly, and then with greater speed, the music began to take over their minds, sending them into a trance-like state, shutting out all thought, all danger, all awareness. Now David and Jenny were moving towards the flat sand, towards the glittering, glimmering sea.

Suddenly they heard voices raised in song and soon the hypnotic rhythm had words.

'Will you dance with the dead, my merry little friends?
Will you dance? Will you dance?
Till your lives do end?
Will you dance with the dead, my merry little friends?
Will you sing? Will you shout?
Until the drowned come all about?'

David was the first to try to break the deadly rhythm, but it wasn't until they were almost at the edge of the lapping sea that he succeeded.

'Stop, Jenny,' he yelled. 'Just stop!'

But she was still moving towards the waves, her hands outstretched, and in the livid light of the moon David could see shapes looming out of the water. Walls. A chimney. A collapsed roof. Then he saw shadows among the ruins, clapping a ghostly rhythm. He could see musicians. He could see dancers. David could see the dead and already Jenny was in the shallows, splashing towards them.

'*Will you dance with the dead, my—*'

'Jenny!' yelled David. 'Stop where you are. Just stop!'

But she was up to her knees now, gazing ahead, her lips moving, her hands still stretching out to the figures among the ruins.

Without trying to attract her attention any more, David ran across the shallows and rugby tackled her, bringing his sister down into the cold water. As they fell, he was sure he knew how Rose had drowned.

'You idiot! What did you go and do that for?' Jenny bellowed at him as David scrambled to his feet. 'I'm soaked!'

'Better soaked than dead.'

'What?' She gazed up at him in bewilderment, as if searching for some half-forgotten memory.

'This is the second time they've had a go at you. It must be because we're psychic. Maybe they're afraid of us.'

David turned to look out to sea, but although he could still see the ruins there were no ghostly shapes standing among them. There was no music, nor was there any singing. Just the sighing of the wavelets over the flat sand.

'What was happening?' Jenny gasped. 'What was I doing?'

'You wanted to dance with the dead,' said David baldly.

'You mean—'

'They were singing to you. They almost got you.'

'Me?'

'You,' he replied firmly. 'They were singing to me as well but I managed to break the spell.'

They ran back across the muddy moonlit sand. The long arms of the breakwaters stretched out beyond the tideline in an attempt to halt the eroding sea, and suddenly Jenny came to a stumbling halt, staring ahead of her.

Words were freshly scrawled in the green slime on the rotting wood of one of the breakwaters. The letters were large and straggling and could have been made by a thin stick – or someone's fingernail.

Even now the wet and pulpy surface was filling them in, but not before the twins caught a glimpse of the message.

DON'T LET CHARLIE DANCE, read the first line, and then the second read: HE MUSTN'T COME. IT'S LONELY OUT HERE.

'It's Rose,' whispered David.

'It's horrible. They took her. She didn't *want* to drown.'

'Neither did any of the people in the church hall that night. Maybe they're all unquiet spirits.'

'What do they want then?' demanded Jenny.

'I don't know,' said David. 'I wish I did.'

CHAPTER FOUR

'I don't know how you got so wet,' said Aunty Betty when the twins returned home shivering to the pub. 'But I suppose you were fooling about on the beach. If only Terry would fool about. But no – all he'll do is sit and watch the television or fish at that jetty, staring out to sea as if he was waiting for his ship to come home.'

What's he really waiting for? wondered David.

They were sitting round the kitchen table drinking cocoa and eating sausage rolls. Next door the TV set thundered.

Both David and Jenny were in their dressing gowns, exhausted by the day's events and almost nodding off to sleep. But David was still determined to ask a few more questions. Jenny's near drowning, the appearance of the Swinton Drowned and his sister's attempted abduction as well as the writing on the breakwater had made him deeply afraid. He knew that Jenny must feel even worse. So far only she had been their victim.

'Have there been a lot of drownings in Swinton?' David asked eventually, sounding rather artificial.

'That's a morbid question,' said Betty briskly.

'I just wondered,' David replied defensively, trying to ignore Jenny's warning look.

'Well, there have been quite a few, but I wouldn't put it down to dancing with the dead.' Aunty Betty gave them a brief and rather strained smile, as if she was trying to rationalise something that she knew she couldn't. 'This coast is really dangerous now. The erosion is serious, and although we're safe this side of the harbour they never were the other – not till that new wall was built. I don't know why – and neither do the experts – but the sea builds right up when you're least expecting it. Almost as if the tide's coming in for the attack.' Then she grinned sheepishly at them both. 'Now I'm talking utter nonsense. I must be as exhausted as you look. I think you should go up to—'

'Did they get a warning?' asked Jenny. 'Those people dancing in the church hall in 1896?'

Betty Todd paused. 'All *I* know is what your grandfather told me and his dad had told him. The tides and currents are so unpredictable here that the town appointed a weather watcher. He had a cottage high up on the cliff and he made a life-long study of the sea and its freak conditions round these parts.' She hesitated. 'His name was Nathaniel and he'd been good at his job as weather watcher right up until the tragedy. His predictions were accurate and folk took avoiding action when necessary whether they were out at sea or on land.' Betty stopped and looked away. 'But what happened next is probably as false as the legend itself.' She seemed reluctant to go on.

'What *did* happen?' Jenny prompted.

'Nathaniel lost his wife to one of the men who were dancing in the church hall. They do say – it's all rubbish of course – but they do say the watcher knew all about the sort of tides and currents that might come together to produce the tidal wave, but he didn't pass the information on because he was so consumed with jealousy and rage.'

'He let them all drown?' asked David incredulously.

'It's just a story, that's all.' Aunty Betty seemed angry with herself for telling them. 'Now I've gone and given you both nightmares.'

A few minutes later the twins held a whispered discussion in Jenny's room which overlooked the beach and the dark sand that led towards the ruins.

'Do you think the Swinton Drowned want vengeance?' asked David. 'Do they want to dance with the living and drag them into the sea in revenge for Nathaniel's betrayal?'

'I don't know,' said Jenny. 'Vengeance is a terrible thing.'

David gazed at her with anxiety. 'I wonder how many people have danced with the dead, since the tidal wave? The drownings would all be put down as accidents, or even suicides.'

Jenny stifled a yawn. 'I'm so tired. I just can't cope with it all.'

'What about Terry?' he persisted. 'He's scared out of his mind, isn't he? That's why he tries to blot it all out with food and TV and fishing.'

'Couldn't we ask him?' said Jenny. 'Say we've been talking it over.'

David was doubtful. 'I don't think he'd go for that. I reckon we've got to lead up to it.'

'How do we do that?'

'Terry must be worried that Charlie *wants* to be taken. Couldn't we make that an excuse to talk?'

'Do you think Rose's communicating with Terry too – telling him she doesn't want Charlie to try and join her?'

'She's had plenty of opportunity.' David went to

the window and looked at the long breakwaters stretching out over the flat wet sand. He shivered. 'It must have been dreadful that night. Dancing away without a care in the world and then having the sea suddenly come sweeping in . . .' He paused. 'That music was so weird,' he went on. 'We *had* to join in. There was no choice. I only just managed to break the spell.'

'I know,' said Jenny with considerable feeling.

David looked up towards the cliffs. 'And all the time the weather watcher had secret knowledge about the tide and the currents. He could see the lights in the village hall. He knew the wave was coming. He just watched them drown. If that's not revenge—' He broke off. 'Do you think his cottage is still up there, on the clifftop?'

'We'll have to go and see,' said Jenny, her eyes closing. 'Let's go up there in the morning,' she said. 'Take a look round.'

David looked at his sister uneasily. He always knew when she was afraid and, besides, he wasn't feeling that good himself about going to sleep.

'You know where I am if you want me in the night.'

'I'm not that thick. You're next door.'

'I could always bring a few blankets in here.'

'I'll be fine.'

David wasn't so sure. Neither was Jenny. But she knew she had to fight back.

CHAPTER FIVE

At first David slept fitfully, but soon he plunged into a much deeper sleep, a sleep that felt menacing, almost suffocating.

Then he heard a strange bubbling sound and began to think that he might be deep under water. From somewhere above, up on the surface, he could just hear his sister's distorted voice.

'David!'

He had the duvet over his head and Jenny was finding it impossible to wake him.

'David!' Her voice was urgent, insistent. He suddenly surfaced and sat up, gasping for air, unsure of where he was.

'Something's happening outside.'

He stared at his sister for a moment and then climbed stiffly out of bed. Jenny went to the window and pulled back the curtains.

David's room also overlooked the beach and by craning their necks they could just see the tideline.

Two shadowy figures were moving towards the ruins and there could be no doubt about their identity. Charlie and Terry strode purposefully across the sand, as if they knew exactly what they were doing.

David tried to pull himself together, but he was still all too aware of the feeling of suffocating, of drowning. 'They'd better not be long,' he mumbled. 'The tide must be on the turn by now.'

Then Terry and Charlie disappeared from sight.

Long slithers of water, oily black in the soft moonlight, crept over the sands, gliding forward ruthlessly, sliding between the weed-hung walls of the ruins, artfully cutting off the way back to the beach.

'They'll be drowned,' whispered Jenny. 'We've got to tell someone.'

Then they heard the hollow booming of the drowned bell and David just suppressed a scream.

Charlie and Terry came into view as the waves were beginning to glide towards them, but neither seemed to notice. Charlie was carrying something. The twins saw him turn his head towards the encroaching tide, coming in faster now, the white foam licking the muddy sand, crests shimmering in the night breeze. Charlie gave a shout, Terry glanced back and they both began to run.

'The tide's going to get them,' gasped Jenny. 'They don't stand a chance.'

Charlie and Terry were running even faster now, trying to beat the sea that was swirling over the sand, a vast sweep of black velvet. David had never seen a tide move so rapidly, and the rolling waves were only a couple of metres behind them.

David felt hot and cold at the same time, while Jenny screwed up her fists so hard that it hurt, her nails digging into the palms of her hands. Charlie staggered for a moment, but Terry grabbed his arm and he managed to regain his stride. Then, just in time, they made the beach and the twins could hear their feet crunching on the pebbles.

The pursuit was over. The tide had lost. But only just.

For a moment the moon seemed incredibly bright, focusing on the waves, the light so fierce that the sea turned momentarily to silver.

Jenny and David watched Charlie and Terry slow down and look cautiously up at the pub, the old man puffing and panting and the overweight Terry doing much the same. He's better off in the sea, thought Jenny. Terry had swum like a seal when he had come to their rescue.

When they had recovered their breath, the old man and the boy began to stumble up the beach towards the Fisherman's Rest and disappeared inside.

The twins listened intently, but it was over twenty minutes before they heard soft footsteps on the stairs.

'Where do you think they've been all this time?' David whispered.

'Charlie was carrying something,' said Jenny. 'Maybe they've hidden it somewhere.' She paused. 'What are we going to do?'

'Talk to Terry,' David replied. 'We've got to find out what he's up to.'

Jenny shivered, unable to banish the image of the racing tide.

'I don't know what Charlie and Terry are doing, but I'm sure it's connected with the Drowned,' he muttered, and Jenny knew he was as afraid as she was.

CHAPTER SIX

Next morning David woke bleary-eyed, having passed the remainder of the night in light, restless and fearful sleep.

He went to the window. It was just after eight and the sun was climbing up into a deep blue sky and the sea was lapping at the pebbles. A lone bather was already ploughing her way out through the waves. Was she aware that the Swinton Drowned were under the sun-sparkling sea, he wondered, or did most people dismiss the idea as a piece of superstition? Then he remembered the framed legend that had been taken out of the snug and hung in the passageway. That meant that at least some of the local people were uneasy. Did they think the Swinton Drowned's desire for revenge was getting stronger? And what had Charlie and Terry taken from the ruins in the night?

David pulled on a T-shirt and jeans and knocked on his sister's door.

'Who is it?' Her voice sounded thin.

'Dave.'

'Come in then.'

She too was standing by the window. When Jenny turned round he could see from her face that she had hardly slept at all.

'Are you all right?' David asked feebly.

'No. I didn't sleep much, did you? I kept thinking the Drowned were coming for me. Third time lucky!'

'No chance.' David tried to sound reassuring. 'We've *got* to talk to Terry. We're out on a limb and in real danger.'

'You don't have to tell me that,' said Jenny miserably.

Downstairs, Aunty Betty was frying bacon.

'I'm making you the usual big breakfast,' she said, giving the twins a beaming smile.

'Is Terry around?' asked David.

'He's sick.'

'Sick?' David looked up at his aunt doubtfully. 'He can't be.'

'I'm afraid he is. He must have got cold swimming about in the sea yesterday. I'm surprised you didn't catch your deaths.'

We almost did, Jenny thought ruefully.

Aunty Betty flipped over the fried bread, not seeming particularly worried about Terry or put out in the least.

'So he's not having breakfast then?'

'Oh well – he said he could manage some scrambled eggs and buttered toast.'

He can't be *that* sick, thought David. But he didn't dare say anything.

'I'm so sorry. Do you want to take *Sunrise* out again? The weather's calmed down and I know you'll be careful.'

That was good of her, thought Jenny. She was sure her own parents would have made a terrible fuss about the capsizing, probably banning them from sailing for weeks. But Aunty Betty seemed to have taken it all in her stride.

'Don't worry about us,' said David. 'We thought we'd take *Sunrise* out this afternoon and go for a walk this morning. Maybe explore the cliffs.'

Taking her cue, Jenny added, 'Does Nathaniel's place still exist?'

'Only the walls. He left the village after the drownings and not before time. The local people burnt his cottage down. Just keep going up the cliff path and you'll come to what's left.'

What *does* she know? wondered Jenny as, surprisingly hungry, she consumed the huge breakfast.

Underneath all that brisk, commonsense warmth, was their aunt a frightened woman?

As the path wound its way up the cliff, a sluggish sea worried at the pebbles below, sunlight dancing on the waves, turning them a crystal green until they burst lazily in a cloud of silver spray.

Betty had packed up a picnic for the twins and loaned them rucksacks. Judging by their weight, she must, as usual, have been generous with the rations. They had already stopped to drink some of her delicious home-made lemonade, which slaked their thirst with just a tangy hint of its original coldness.

Gulls wheeled across the sea, mewing and then diving down to fish, while cormorants gathered under the cliff face, standing in sentinel lines, gazing out at the horizon.

The Swinton Drowned seemed light years away on this sunlit morning. Yet when Jenny saw a strip of sand beneath the pebbles and realised the tide was beginning to turn, even in the sunlight, she felt uneasy.

'Do you think Rose got caught by the tide?' The idea had suddenly come into her head and Jenny wondered what David thought about it.

'That's interesting,' he replied bleakly.

'It's horrible,' she said indignantly. 'Think of

what we saw last night. The water came darting in as if it had tentacles. Suppose poor Rose had gone out to the ruins and misjudged the tide, like Charlie and Terry did last night. Suppose she couldn't run fast enough?' She shivered. 'I don't know which is worse. The sea or the Drowned. They're both vindictive.'

The twins walked on up in silence, both pre-occupied with their own thoughts, just occasionally glancing down at the sea. A fishing boat was motoring past the cliffs, the steady chugging of its engine a comforting sound. Jenny remembered the booming of the bell and suddenly felt a dread about sailing over drowned Swinton again.

'Do we *have* to go out in *Sunrise* this afternoon?'

'If we don't, we'll never get back in her again,' David assured her. 'It'll be like getting on again after falling off a horse. If we don't do it fast, we'll never make it.' He paused and forced himself to be more honest. 'I'm feeling scared too, particularly as the tide's going out.'

'I know.' Jenny turned to reassure him, grateful for David's truthfulness. It was a quality in him that she knew she could always rely on. 'I'm sorry to be chicken.'

'You're not.' Then he said more convincingly, 'Well, if you are, so am I. I don't want to sail over that church either, but I feel we've *got* to do it.'

Jenny nodded uneasily. Why was David so compelled to take out *Sunrise*? She shivered at her choice of the word compelled. But there was something about David's determination that went beyond common sense.

The path was climbing more steeply now until it finally reached the headland.

'This is it. This is where Nathaniel's house was,' Jenny exclaimed.

But all that remained was a low and occasionally broken stone wall with smooth sheep-shorn turf both inside and out.

'He must have felt like a god, looking down on all those tiny people and being responsible for their fate,' Jenny continued. She was silent for a while and then she said, 'When his wife left him, maybe Nathaniel felt he was drowning ants.'

There were people moving about on the harbour wall and traffic buzzed in the streets of the town that stretched right back as far as the railway station, with clusters of old buildings, spoilt here and there by a modern block of flats or a supermarket. The whole of Swinton looked like a set of building blocks that could be knocked aside by some giant hand. Had it seemed as vulnerable to the vengeful Nathaniel?

'Let's have the picnic here,' said David. 'You can't believe in ghosts in the sunlight, can you?'

'It all looks so innocent, doesn't it?' Jenny agreed. 'But when the tide goes out and all that muddy sand is uncovered as well as the ruins – it's another place.'

As she spoke, Jenny saw a large piece of wood drifting through the waves. She watched its journey towards the shore idly, letting her mind drift as well, thankfully relaxed. The driftwood had a distinctive shape that reminded her of something she couldn't quite remember.

David had stopped eating and was staring down at the almost unruffled surface of the sea where little darts of sunlight glistened. 'Isn't that a coffin lid?' he asked quietly, and then turned to Jenny in mounting concern. 'I mean – it can't be, can it?'

CHAPTER SEVEN

Jenny gazed at the object intently as the oblong piece of wood bobbed up and down. 'I don't know,' she said. 'It could be anything.' She was deliberately keeping calm, pushing away the unpleasant thoughts. When the tidal wave hit the church it must also have damaged the churchyard. The living had drowned while they danced, but had the dead been exhumed? Had coffins actually been sucked out of their graves? Although she knew they would have rotted, her mind wouldn't let go of the gruesome picture.

'It's heading for the beach,' David said dolefully.

The driftwood was on such a consistent course that Jenny began to think it was being propelled. 'I don't believe this,' she said briskly, covering up her alarm. 'It's heading for that breakwater over there.'

Sure enough it headed straight through the waves for the jagged wood. The impact was not long in coming, although they could hear nothing from where they were.

'It's got wedged,' said David.

There was a long silence, eventually broken by Jenny.

'Should we – should we go down and take a look?'

'OK.' David drained the last of his lemonade. 'Might as well.' He was elaborately casual. 'Then we'll take out *Sunrise*.'

They ran down the cliff path although neither of them really wanted to arrive at the beach. The sun had gone behind a cloud and without its warmth and light the sea had turned a sullen grey green.

There were quite a few would-be sunbathers on the pebbles now, largely families with small children who were splashing about in the shallows or digging in the sand that had been left by the tide. Some of them were gazing up in irritation at the cloud that covered the sun.

No one was taking any interest in the driftwood, but as they got nearer Jenny was forced to admit that it did look like a coffin lid.

Finally, out of breath and anxious, they arrived on the beach and scrunched over the pebbles towards the breakwater. The driftwood had come to a halt at the very end, and they began to scramble over the wet and slippery surface to take a closer look. Jenny went first, with David close behind, and eventually they came alongside what they were now sure was the tarnished and pulpy-looking lid of a coffin, some of which had rotted away.

'I don't like this,' whispered Jenny, crouching over the lid, gazing down at it and then taking a covert glance at the beach. But no one seemed to be looking in their direction.

'Wait a minute,' said David suddenly. 'There's something scratched on the surface.'

Jenny clambered even further along the break-water to get a better view. Once again David followed, his feet slipping on the thickly encrusted seaweed.

'What does it say?' he asked.

'It's hard to read.' Jenny was silent for some time, staring down as if she couldn't believe her own eyes. 'No. It can't be!' She began to shake and her face was rigid with a kind of angry fear.

'Come on!' said David with impatience.

'It says – I *think* it says – WE'LL TAKE A CHILD FOR THE HARM YOU DO.'

'They're threatening us.' Jenny's voice was so thin that her twin could hardly make out what she was saying.

'What does it mean – for the harm you do?'

asked David hesitantly.

'They think we're interfering.' Jenny swallowed. 'We'll take a child for the harm you do,' she repeated.

'Do you think it's meant for us, or could it be for Terry and Charlie?' David clutched at the notion. 'I mean, they're the ones who've been poking about in the ruins – *and* taking things. Just because we saw this coming in, doesn't mean to say it's for us.' Then he felt ashamed of himself for wishing the threat was meant for someone else.

Jenny shrugged. It was impossible to tell who the message on the coffin lid was meant for, but it was unnerving, particularly after all that had happened, and especially to her. Again she felt the silky stuff wrapping itself tightly around her ankles, dragging her down into the cold depths. She gazed out to the red marker buoy and shuddered.

David glanced back at the beach and said softly, 'We're being watched.'

'Who by?' Jenny whipped round and almost lost her balance. She just managed to save herself as she saw a young priest smiling at her, standing on the edge of the pebbles.

'It must be the vicar,' said David. 'What does he want?'

'Maybe he's recognised the coffin lid,' suggested

Jenny. 'I mean – in his business he must know one when he sees one.'

'Jenny and David Golding?' The young man was short and energetic looking, dressed in a sports jacket and flannels with a white dog collar and a highly polished pair of brown brogues. 'I'm the Reverend Alan Moore. Mrs Todd – your aunt – said you'd be on the beach. I was wondering if you'd like to join the Happy Wanderers?'

'What's that?' asked David. 'A football club?'

'Er – not exactly. More like a holiday youth club. Of course we do kick a ball around.' He caught Jenny's eye, and added quickly, 'And there's lots of things for the girls to do.'

'What things?' she asked suspiciously.

'Mask-making – and – er – dressing-up competitions.'

Jenny gave him a chilly smile.

'Your aunt was worried that you might be getting bored,' said the Reverend Moore. 'And I'm always anxious to increase the Happy Wanderers.'

'How many members have you got?' asked David.

'Just under a dozen, so as you can imagine I'd like a few more.'

'Sorry,' said Jenny. 'We go sailing most days.'

'With your cousin Terry?'

'He's gone off the sea,' stated David baldly.

'That's because of the tragedy.'

'Probably,' said Jenny, not wanting to commit herself.

The young vicar caught sight of the driftwood, still stuck up against the breakwater. 'Wait a minute. That looks just like a coffin lid.' He laughed uneasily.

David was suddenly determined to put him off, although he couldn't think why. 'It's the shape that's all. Are you new here?'

'I've been here six months. Clannish sort of place though. My predecessor had been here for twenty years and people don't like changes, do they? They're also very superstitious. Look at this dancing with the dead business.' The vicar hesitated, obviously regretting having been so outspoken.

'Do you believe in the legend?' asked Jenny, seizing her opportunity.

'Of course I don't, but I can't ignore the strong belief some of the old people have here – particularly the fishermen.'

'What do you mean?'

'I don't want to fill your heads with silly, frightening stories.'

'We know about this already,' said David craftily. 'Because of Rose.'

'Of course. I'm so sorry. You know, I've often thought a service on the beach might be a good thing.'

'An exorcism?' David asked with relish.

'I was thinking of a blessing. It might put paid to some of this superstitious nonsense I keep hearing. But I'm not getting much backing from the Parochial Church Council.' He was staring out to sea again, and when David and Jenny turned to follow his gaze they saw the scarred and pitted pulpy wood of the coffin lid suddenly free itself from the breakwater and swiftly float away. 'That tide's got a pretty strong pull today.' He turned back to them. There was something resolute about the Reverend Moore that was reassuring, David thought. But he's a stranger here, like us. And strangers aren't welcome.

'I liked him, didn't you?' said Jenny as they watched the vicar stride briskly along the beach to the harbour.

'Yes. But I'm not joining the Happy Wanderers.'

'Neither am I.'

'I'm dreading tonight, aren't you?' David was looking really worried. 'I'm sure that warning was meant for us.'

'You don't really mean to take *Sunrise* out this

afternoon, do you?' Jenny was almost pleading. 'I don't think I could bear to go through that again. Ever. I don't mind sailing. But not here.' She wondered if David was going to insist – or the Drowned were going to compel him to insist. It was a strange notion, but a horrible one. Could they have got into her brother's head? Could the Drowned be influencing him in some way? She tried to dismiss the idea. 'They'll pull me down,' she continued with a half-sob.

Then David said abruptly, 'I don't think I want to take *Sunrise* out either.' Jenny felt a surge of relief. It was as if he had unknowingly used all his willpower to fight them off. 'Not till we've really got to grips with all this.'

'I tell you what,' she said. 'Let's go and find Terry.'

'He's ill.'

'He's afraid,' she corrected David firmly. 'We can tell Aunty Betty that we want to go in and cheer him up. That's if she's there, of course.'

'What if she isn't?' asked David.

'We'll just barge in. Catch him at a disadvantage.'

Unfortunately, the twins' plan went wrong directly they got back to the Fisherman's Rest.

'Did you meet the vicar?' asked Aunty Betty as she came down the passageway from the bar.

'Yes,' said Jenny. 'He's nice.'

'I thought you'd like to join his club. I've been afraid you might get bored. What with Terry being so difficult.'

'No thanks,' replied David abruptly.

'Oh dear—'

'It just isn't us,' explained Jenny. 'We'd much rather work on Terry.' Without giving her aunt a chance to reply, she hurried on. 'I thought we'd look in on him. Have a chat. Try to cheer him up.'

'I'm afraid you can't do that,' said Aunty Betty. 'I've just sent him up to the surgery – or rather his dad has.'

'That's right,' said Uncle Trevor, overhearing as he came in from the bar. 'Either he's ill or he's not ill. I reckon the doctor's the best person to find out. I'm not going to have that lad malingering on a nice sunny day like today.' He grinned and winked at the twins as he passed by. 'Personally I hope the doc puts a boot up his backside. That's the only medicine our Terry understands.'

'Aren't you taking out *Sunrise*?' asked Aunty Betty.

'We thought we'd check out the rigging and sail her tomorrow,' Jenny improvised quickly. 'We're a bit tired after all that walking.'

'You take it easy.' She smiled at them warmly. 'It's nice to see a couple of kids with some spirit in them.'

When their aunt and uncle had gone back into the bar, Jenny gave David a helpless smile. 'I reckon I've got more spirit in me than you.'

Her eyes were full of tears and David scowled. 'Don't worry, Jenny. They're not going to get you. They're not going to get either of us.'

But his words had a hollow ring as they both gazed at the print on the pub wall showing the tidal wave enveloping St Stephen's.

CHAPTER EIGHT

That afternoon the tide was out and the Swinton ruins were exposed once again. Jenny and David stood on the jetty looking across the harbour to the beach beyond and at the gaunt figure of Charlie Hamilton walking purposefully towards the weed-hung remains of the drowned village.

'Why don't we join him?' Jenny suggested. 'I bet loads of tourists go out there. Let's stroll across and see what he's up to?'

'Won't he think we're spying on him?' asked David anxiously. 'We don't want to put his back up. We might need his help.'

'We're tourists. The drowned village is a tourist attraction. We've got every right to go and take a look. In fact, it would seem very odd if we didn't.'

'All right,' said David. 'You've talked me into it. But be careful. Don't start upsetting him.'

'As if I would,' replied Jenny indignantly.

By the time they got to the beach there were

quite a few holidaymakers walking across the wet sand. In the afternoon sunlight, the ruins looked dull and ordinary – just a few seawrack-covered and barnacle-encrusted humps. It was impossible to get inside them and even the holidaymakers soon lost interest and begin to head back to the shore.

One of the ruined cottages, larger than the others, lay a little further out to sea across a patch of soggy-looking sand which everyone had avoided. Charlie, however, who had been lost to sight for some time, suddenly appeared from the furthest ruin in a pair of waders, a bag slung over his back. In fact he arrived so unexpectedly that the twins didn't have time to stop staring.

'What you two doing then?' A frown seared Charlie's craggy face.

'Just taking a look,' said Jenny.

'Nothing to see.'

'No. There isn't much,' agreed David rather too quickly. 'Bit of a waste of time.'

'That was my family home,' said Charlie with a kind of gloomy pride.

'The ruin you've just come out of?' asked David and then looked as if he wished he hadn't spoken. Jenny wished he hadn't either.

'I often go in there,' he snapped. 'It's my right.'

'Of course it is,' said Jenny sympathetically.

'Like to keep a link with the past,' Charlie muttered. 'Only a few stones left, but I still like to stand there and remember my Rose. Maybe her spirit drifts in there on the tide. That's what I like to think. You'll reckon I'm an old fool, but it gives me a bit of comfort.'

'Can *we* go in there?' asked David.

'No chance. There's shifting sand. You'd need waders. No one goes there now.' Charlie looked at David with some hostility. 'So don't let me catch you trying.'

'What about the old St Stephen's?' asked Jenny uncertainly.

'What about it?'

'Is it ever uncovered?'

Charlie shook his head. 'The church lies in a hollow in deep water. No tide ever uncovers St Stephen's.'

'Have divers ever been down there?'

'Dozens of times. But they won't find anything. Now, I've got to get going. The Todds'll be needing me at the Fisherman's Rest. Remember what I said, you two, that old place is dangerous. Got it?'

'Got it,' replied Jenny.

'I'd like to know what he had in that bag,' said David, training his eyes on Charlie's retreating figure.

'Let's give him some time,' suggested Jenny. 'He said he had to work in the pub. Maybe while Charlie's out of the way in the bar we could take a quick look in the cellars – see if there's anything there. That's the most likely hiding place. But we'll have to be really careful no one finds us snooping.'

'Particularly Charlie,' observed David. 'I get a feeling he's easily upset.'

Fifteen minutes later the twins wandered back into the kitchen and, for once, Aunty Betty didn't seem to be around.

'I'll see if Charlie's safely behind the bar,' said Jenny.

She wasn't away long and when she returned she was in a cool and confident mood.

'Charlie's talking to a fisherman. It looks like one of those conversations that could take a while.'

'Let's hope he doesn't need to come down to the cellar,' said David, 'or we'll have dropped ourselves right in it.'

They crept cautiously down the passage that linked the kitchen with the saloon bar. Halfway down, the cellar door was slightly open.

'Let's go,' hissed David, but the steps were in darkness and Jenny spent some time fumbling for the light switch. When she found it, the neon strip seemed to shine too hard and too bright.

Leaving the door ajar, the twins hurried furtively down.

Barrels of beer were the main contents, with a few racks of wine and bottles of soft drinks. Matted cobwebs hung from the ceiling and there were signs of active life in their silky threads. David shuddered. He couldn't stand spiders.

'You take that side and I'll take the other,' he said. 'We'll have to work fast.'

Frantic minutes later, they were still searching but nothing had come to light.

Then Jenny saw that a mass of thick cobwebs had been disturbed. They hung limply to one side, exposing a small wooden door whose paint had almost completely flaked away. She pulled at the handle and the door opened to reveal a space that might once have been a cold store. At first it seemed empty, but as her fingers groped around she found a collection of lumpy objects at the back.

'David,' she called softly. 'Come over here.'

By the time he had joined her, Jenny had pulled out an object which was heavily encrusted with barnacles.

'What is it?' she whispered.

'I reckon it *was* a harmonica,' replied David.

There were three more, and then, at the very back, something much bigger. All smelt strongly of brine.

'It's a concertina,' said Jenny. 'We've got four harmonicas and a concertina. Maybe that's what he was bringing up the beach when he was with Terry. What's Charlie hidden them here for? You couldn't play any of them.'

'He must have found them in that cottage – or what's left of it.'

'So?' said Jenny.

'Maybe Charlie reckons he could flog them to a museum.'

'He'd be lucky.'

The twins stared down at the battered instruments, feeling disappointed with their find.

'Let's shove them back.' But as Jenny spoke they heard the sound of footsteps slowly descending the cellar stairs.

She quickly replaced the instruments, making a scraping sound, and David closed his eyes against the grim realisation of what was going to happen next. It's a fair cop, he said to himself.

'What have you got there?' Terry sounded triumphant; his heavy bulk seemed to fill the low, narrow cellar. 'You're not meant to be down here.'

'We were just—' David began and then came to a stumbling halt.

'Just what?'

'Hanging around.' David said lamely.

Jenny, however, decided to seize the opportunity. 'We're worried about Charlie,' she said. 'Certain things have been happening we'd like to talk to you about – if you're interested that is.'

A cloudy look came into Terry's eyes. 'What do you mean?' he asked in a choked voice, backing away slightly as if he had been physically threatened.

'Charlie's been collecting stuff,' said David. He went back to the cold store and pulled out one of the barnacle-encrusted harmonicas. 'There're more of these and a concertina. We think they came from his family's ruined cottage. So why's he bringing them back here?' Terry didn't reply and David added, 'You must have some idea. We saw you with him on the sands last night.'

'Yes,' said Terry. He now looked desperately afraid. 'I was with him.' He turned away and the twins realised he was almost in tears. 'I can't stand this any longer.'

'Stand what?' demanded David.

'Waiting.'

'For what?'

'The dead, of course. The drowned dead. I've been waiting for them all year. Ever since Rose died.'

CHAPTER NINE

The three of them left the cellar and walked out into the daylight, sitting down on the jetty in the mellow late afternoon sunshine. The sea was calm and the weather sultry, with dark clouds hovering on a distant horizon.

'I thought you were ill,' said David flatly.

'I wasn't ill. I was scared. So scared I couldn't think of anything else.' Terry paused and gazed at the twins with a strange glitter in his eyes. 'Don't you understand? They're coming tonight. The Drowned are coming.' He paused again and then whispered, 'They're going to take me away.'

David and Jenny gazed at their cousin in mounting horror.

'Why do you think that?' demanded Jenny.

'I'll show you why.' Terry jumped to his feet and leant over the edge of the jetty, pulling out from a crevice a small piece of driftwood. On the side was scratched: WE'LL TAKE A CHILD FOR

THE HARM HE DID.

'How long have you had this?' Jenny asked shakily.

'Ever since last year. It was floating in the water under this jetty the day after Rose drowned. I know it was meant for me.'

'*How* do you know?' asked David. 'It doesn't have your name on.'

'We're his descendants. I bet Mum didn't mention the weather watcher's full name. It was Nathaniel Todd.'

There was a long silence. The Swinton Drowned had suddenly come horribly close to home.

Then Terry said, 'Dad and Mum don't talk about it even between themselves. Dad's really set himself up not to believe in the Drowned, despite what happened to Rose. Mum *does* believe. I'm sure she does. But even she still tries to sweep it all away.'

Terry's words tumbled over each other in his hurry to tell the twins everything. No wonder, thought David. He's been bottling it up for a year with no one to talk to but a half-crazy old man.

'Not many people know that the wife who deserted Nathaniel had a child. When she was drowned and he left Swinton, the boy went into a workhouse. As I said, in their different ways Dad and Mum try to dismiss the legend as a load of rubbish, but *I* don't think it is. Not after Rose. Not after this. The Swinton Drowned want revenge. They want the descendants.'

'But Rose wasn't one, was she?' asked Jenny. 'The Drowned have gone wider than just grabbing Nathaniel's descendants.'

Terry shook his head. 'She was just a victim – in the wrong place at the wrong time. I reckon they just want people who are much loved,' he said. 'After all, they had to leave their loved ones behind.'

Jenny thought of her own parents and shuddered.

'But what about your family?' demanded David.

'One of my great-uncles was drowned when he was a kid and then later an uncle and an aunt. Now it's my turn.'

'You're not alone,' said Jenny quietly.

'Don't get you.' Terry was bewildered.

She began to tell him about the bell and the capsize again, and the song they had heard and the coffin lid with its inscription. She then told Terry about the Reverend Moore.

Although he listened, he seemed hardly able to take in what Jenny was talking about. Terry was obviously obsessed by the threat to himself, the threat that was now only hours away. Nor did he approve of the vicar's campaign to organise a blessing of the waters. 'I wish he'd leave it alone. The Drowned will think Swinton's going to war against them. They'll just get stronger.'

'You've overlooked something,' snapped Jenny. 'Something important.'

'What?' demanded Terry ungraciously.

'That coffin lid. It was meant for us – not you. *We* were being warned as well. It's not just you. We're a threat to the Drowned too, and that's because we're psychic.' Jenny began to tell Terry about the special gift that she and David had kept secret, the gift that had got them into so much trouble in the past, the gift that the Swinton Drowned had clearly recognised. At last Terry seemed to understand.

'Then you *can* help! You can help Charlie – *and* me!'

'What was he doing, collecting all those old instruments?' asked David.

'He's crazy. All he wants is for the Drowned to take him so he can be with Rose. Anyway, Charlie discovered these harmonicas and concertinas in a built-in cupboard, part of the chimney breast in the ruins of his father's cottage. He was a musician and led the band for the dance. They were spares, I suppose. Charlie's often been poking about in there since Rose drowned. Then he found that lot. He's planning to offer the instruments to the Drowned tonight, and in return he says they'll have to take him. I know it's a weird idea but he believes in it. We've got to stop him. He's not responsible for his own actions.' Terry paused for a moment, blinking back the tears. 'We need him. *I* need him. He's always been like a grandfather to me, just like Rose was a grandmother. Now she's gone, I can't lose Charlie as well!'

'We've got to find out what might help the Drowned – that's the only way we'll be able to help him,' said David. 'They haven't had a proper burial – and they're in limbo. Shouldn't the vicar be given a chance?'

'No one in Swinton would wear that,' muttered Terry.

'Why not?'

'Because he's not one of us. He makes it sound too easy. They won't accept the vicar can just get rid of the Swinton Drowned with a few prayers.'

David desperately searched for an alternative. 'We don't have to wait here and find ourselves dancing with the dead. We could leave and spend the night away. If you've got a tent, we could go camping. They only come up on the beach, don't they?'

'No,' said Terry bleakly. 'They're more powerful than that. They've been seen in the town and beyond. Anyway – I can't desert Charlie. And he'd never leave.'

'Neither can I,' said Jenny. 'This situation's got to be resolved. Have you tried to talk Charlie out of his crazy idea?'

Terry nodded. 'You bet I have. That's why I walked out to the ruins with him last night. But he wouldn't listen – he just wants to be with Rose. He's still half mad with grief.'

'Have you seen her?' asked David.

'No. I wish I had. Charlie hasn't either, but he says he hears her calling to him from the sea.'

We have, thought Jenny, wondering if they should tell Terry or not.

'Wait a minute!' There was a surge of renewed hope in Terry's voice.

'What is it?' asked David warily.

'You say you're psychic. Both of you?'

'So it seems.' Jenny was equally uncomfortable. What was Terry building up to?

'You've got these special powers. Couldn't *you* contact the Drowned and ask them to spare Charlie?' Terry was suddenly and desperately optimistic.

71

'They haven't said they want him yet,' said David haltingly.

'He wants *them*. If he joins the dance, they're bound to take him. Plead with them. They can't *all* be evil. There must be some of them who might be sympathetic, who might show some mercy.'

He has a point, thought David.

We've never done this before, Jenny told herself. The dead have always contacted us. We've never tried to contact them.

'Please,' said Terry urgently.

The Drowned have already proved hostile, thought David. Suppose we play into their dead hands by contacting them?

'All right,' said Jenny. 'We'll have a go.'

The tide seemed to be rushing out, leaving acres of flat, wet sand and the seaweed-covered humps of the ruins.

'When?' asked Terry.

'What time does the tide turn?' Jenny was as scared as David now, but they were both convinced that they must try to intervene.

'Not till ten.'

'Is that when the Drowned come?' asked David fearfully. 'On the turn of the tide?'

'That's what they say,' replied Terry quietly.

'We don't want to go then. It's too dangerous.'

Jenny tried to sound more confident. 'We'll walk across the sand after tea and try to make contact.'

'What on earth are we going to say to them?'

'We'll have to play it by ear I suppose,' suggested Jenny uneasily.

'Great,' replied David miserably.

'And I'm coming with you.' Terry had obviously made a sudden decision.

'You don't have to.'

'Oh yes he does,' snapped David. 'After all, it was *his* idea.'

CHAPTER TEN

Betty and Trevor Todd were delighted to discover that Terry had become so much more friendly with David and Jenny. 'I'm going to take them out in *Sunrise* tomorrow,' he told his astounded parents at teatime. 'Not that I can teach them anything.'

'We still managed to capsize,' admitted Jenny who didn't in the least want to go out in *Sunrise*, but Trevor swept that aside.

'To capsize is to learn,' he said. 'And you got yourselves out of trouble.'

'They'd have done it without me,' said Terry. Now that he had come out of his shell, he seemed anxious to reach his parents, make them think he was someone again. But Jenny knew that he didn't have to try so hard. Betty and Trevor were so pleased that their son had begun to get back to his old self that they would have agreed with anything he said. A distant roll of thunder silenced them all for a moment. The atmosphere was sultry.

Betty's happy face increased David's sense of responsibility. If they couldn't pull off pleading with the Drowned and Charlie was taken, then Terry could so easily revert to his depressed state.

It was unfortunate that Uncle Trevor got too confident and began to joke about the anniversary. There was no doubt, however, that he was still deliberately trying to make light of it all, to try and prove to his son that the family curse was nothing more than superstition.

'So – tonight's the night, eh? Dancing with the dead and all that. I wonder how many people in this town are going to lock their doors and secure their windows? Too many, I'd reckon. I don't suppose you twins know that I'm a descendant of Nathaniel's?' He gave a burst of hearty laughter, but Aunty Betty was watching him as anxiously as she might watch a sick child. 'Mark you, I don't let that get about too much. It might be bad for business, but I don't mind telling you two because I'm sure you won't go round shouting your heads off, although all the locals know, of course. But I've never believed in that stupid legend. Never. What happened to Rose was just a coincidence. A very tragic coincidence because it got a few more believers again – including Charlie.'

No wonder superstitions build up, thought

Jenny, if people can't separate the truth from a lie. But then she realised it wasn't a lie. It was only people like Uncle Trevor who were determined to believe that the dead didn't dance, and she had the impression that despite all the bluster he was really frightened.

'I think we ought to keep an eye on Charlie tonight,' said Aunty Betty, her pleasure in Terry's recovery fading in the face of a new danger.

'He'll be in the bar with me until closing time. Then I'll lock the old devil into his room,' said Uncle Trevor with a return to his forced joviality.

Another roll of thunder suddenly cracked out, nearer this time.

Aunty Betty gave her husband a covert glance, as if they had already discussed the problem of Charlie and she was wondering how much to admit. But whether that meant she believed in dancing with the dead or was genuinely worried about the possibility of Charlie trying to commit suicide was not at all clear.

'Rose and Charlie had become part of our family,' she continued. 'They were loved by us all.' There was a long, emotional silence which was eventually filled by Terry.

'Don't worry, Mum,' he said abruptly. 'We're going to keep Charlie safe. All of us. You'll see.'

'Where are you lot going?' asked Uncle Trevor as he walked towards the bar and saw Jenny, David and Terry making for the back door. Lightning lit the kitchen with a pale and livid light as it ripped across the sky.

'Just out for a stroll.'

'Be careful,' he said. 'Don't start walking out to sea later on. That tide's going to turn fast.'

'Is the old church *ever* exposed?' asked David, trying to see if his uncle might know any more than Charlie.

'Never. St Stephen's was in a dip, and the cottages were on higher ground. Not that it did them much good.'

'How near was the hall to the church? Just a few metres away?'

'Yes. They didn't stand a chance. I'm afraid my ancestor allowed them to suffer a terrible fate. As Terry may have told you, he did a runner, leaving his boy behind to face poverty. It was a right mess all round.' Uncle Trevor paused. 'Even the lowest tide's not going to uncover St Stephen's. Now, I *must* get on. If you see Charlie walking out to sea, tell him he'll get the sack if he doesn't turn round right away. I'm short-handed enough in the bar these days.' He boomed with the same hearty, uneasy laughter and hurried away.

'Dad's trying not to believe, but I reckon he's doing a cover-up like Mum.' Despite this, Terry seemed buoyant. 'Since you two turned up I feel as if I've got some hope at last. It's been a long year – and I've hated every moment of it. Keep Charlie safe,' he pleaded. Then he brightened still further. 'Do you reckon I'll see her?' he asked hesitantly.

'Who?' asked David in confusion.

'Rose, of course. I mean, if you can contact the dead – can't you raise them too?'

'No,' said Jenny vehemently. 'I don't even know if we can reach them. We've never done anything like this before. They've always come to us.'

'So if you're joining us,' David spoke abruptly, 'keep your mouth shut and your eyes open.'

The sand gleamed in the stormy light, soft and treacherous, the ruins looking like crouching sea monsters from the dawn of time. The tide was a long way out and the beach was deserted.

'It's as if they *all* believe,' said David gloomily. 'Holidaymakers and locals alike.'

The storm had still not broken and the humid heat had intensified to such an extent that they all three began to sweat profusely. The clouds above them were a bruised, purplish-blue colour, and from a long way off now they could hear the distant rumble of thunder.

A stiff breeze was blowing off the sea and there was a strong smell of seaweed.

'I don't think it's superstition,' said Terry, trying to be rational. 'It's the weather. No one wants to get caught in a downpour.'

'What time did you say the tide was going to turn?' Jenny asked, looking at her watch. 'It's just on eight.'

'Another couple of hours yet,' said David unhappily. 'How *do* you reach the Drowned anyway? Give them a shout?'

Jenny looked at him doubtfully. She had no idea what they should do. Worst of all, however, she had the feeling that neither she nor David would have to *do* anything. They would be contacted.

Terry was leading now, full of new confidence, striding over the sand. Already they were past the last of the ruined cottages that had been Charlie's family home. Now the going was much softer and David and Jenny realised that none of them had brought waders. How far down would they sink? But the twins soon discovered that Charlie had been exaggerating, for they only sank up to their ankles, and although progress was difficult they managed to keep going.

'How far?' yelled David, for Terry had now drawn quite a distance ahead of them.

'To the edge of the sea,' he shouted back. His bulky figure looked purposeful, even protective; there was something very reassuring about him now that he was able to be more hopeful, to leave his paralysing fear behind.

But then David realised that this was because Terry was relying on them completely. It was a heavy responsibility.

'I hope he's right about the tide,' muttered Jenny.

'It's still going out,' David reassured her. 'Look.'

The retreating sea had exposed a cluster of rocks cratered by the ebb and flow of the tide to form large, dark pools.

Terry had stopped and was gazing down into one of them. 'I've never seen the tide go out so far before,' he said as the twins joined him. He sounded afraid and his new-found confidence seemed to have abruptly disappeared.

Reluctantly they moved on over sand that was much firmer and flatter, but when they reached the edge of the sea they could see that there was a shelf plunging down into dark, lapping water.

'There's the red marker buoy out there.'

'If the water's so deep, how could we see the spire so clearly?'

'I don't know,' replied Terry uneasily. 'I never sailed anywhere near that awful place. I always kept away – like all the locals do.'

'Rose contacted us to stop Charlie being so stupid, but maybe the Drowned want something we might be able to give them.'

'You're not going to help them take me, are you?' said Terry, sounding terrified. Were David and Jenny agents for the Drowned, sent to lure him to his death?

'Of course not,' Jenny replied. 'You know we're—'

'What's that?' broke in David. 'What's that – kind of scurrying sound?'

When they looked back, the black tide pools were teeming with life, and large crabs were already out on the wet sand, scuttling towards them, pincers waving, stalk eyes purposeful.

CHAPTER ELEVEN

'They're trying to cut us off,' yelled David. 'They want to force us into the sea.'

A slight breeze had sprung up and the seaweed in the ruins behind them shivered and slapped. Then a familiar hollow booming sound began. As it did so a silver surge of water rushed towards them, curling round their ankles. The tide was not just cold but strong, its watery tentacles entrapping them, pulling hard towards the sea.

'Did you hear the bell?' asked David. 'Can you hear it now?'

'Yes.' Terry was frantic. 'I can hear it.'

They were silent now, watching the crabs scurrying across the sand towards them with a terrible sense of purpose while the tide still wrenched icily at their feet.

Terry was already moving slowly backwards, step by step, nearer and nearer to the water, while the twins stood their ground, holding out against the sea and their horror of the crabs which had come to a halt, their antennae waving. They were slate grey in colour with long legs that revolted David but had clearly terrified Terry.

'They're a kind of spider crab,' he yelled. 'I couldn't stand being touched by them.'

Neither can we, thought Jenny, the irritation only temporarily masking her revulsion. Didn't Terry think about anyone except himself? Then she remembered that he had been living with his fear for a very long time.

'Stop moving back,' she cried out. 'There's a shelf. The church is waiting for us. That's why the crabs are here. They're going to drive us into the sea.'

David took a chance, ran over to Terry and grabbed at his arm. But the other boy was strong and determined and David knew that if he hung on much longer he would be dragged towards the abyss as well.

Meanwhile the hollow booming continued, muffled but urgent. When it stopped the tide tightened yet again, curling even more strongly around their ankles.

The crabs waited for a moment and then, as if at some unknown signal, turned and scuttled back to the dark rockpools.

Terry came to a swaying halt. He was on the very edge of the shelf, the wavelets tumbling around his ankles.

'It's OK,' said David. 'They've gone.'

'They'll come back.' Terry gave a little whimper, his big body shaking. Then he jerked violently and screamed.

'*Now* what's the matter?' asked David.

Terry kicked out several times and screamed again. 'Something's round my ankles,' he shouted. 'I can't get it off.'

Jenny joined them at the tideline. The water was very cold in the slapping wavelets.

'I can't see anything,' she said, gazing down. 'It must be the tide still. It's very strong.'

'Feels like silky weed,' yelled Terry.

'Silk?' repeated Jenny in horror. 'Did you say—'

Then Terry fell over into the waves and to their horror the twins saw him being sucked towards the pit. The hollow booming of the bell began again, this time sounding louder and triumphant.

Without hesitation, David and Jenny both ran into the numbing cold of the shallows, each grabbing one of Terry's legs, trying to pull him back.

David's hand came into contact with the all too familiar slimy material and he could see the long white silk that was wrapped around Terry's ankles.

He tried to tear it away, but it wound itself around even more tightly and would have grabbed at his own hand if he hadn't reacted quickly.

'Give me your knife!' But as David yelled at Terry another sheet of the silky stuff shot up, covering his pockets.

'I can't reach it,' sobbed Terry. 'You've got to get this thing off me.' The twins were still holding him stationary, but the silky binding around his ankle was dragging strongly.

David tried to think fast, but there was nothing sharp in the seawrack that he could see, and anyway there was the danger of cutting Terry badly if he used a bit of broken tin. He clung on desperately; yet, despite their combined weight, Terry was now being dragged into deeper water and the twins were going with him.

The rock on the edge of the tidal shelf was not exactly jagged but was certainly hard. David thought he might be able to wear the sheet through by rubbing it against the surface.

'Try and keep him steady,' he shouted at Jenny.

'How do I do that?'

'Grab him round the waist.'

Jenny did as she was told, but she wasn't strong enough to hold Terry. Slowly, relentlessly, they were being drawn towards the edge of the pit.

Then the dragging abruptly stopped.

'What's happened?'

'I'm rubbing this sheet thing against the rock. It's beginning to fray.' David gasped with pain as the silk suddenly unravelled, whipping him painfully across the face as it raced out beyond Terry and Jenny into deeper water.

'It wasn't like silk,' muttered David.

'What do you mean?' panted Jenny.

'It was more like skin,' he said. 'Horrible, slimy, Drowned human skin.'

Stumbling, Terry, David and Jenny ran past the rockpools. Terry kept whimpering, hardly able to believe what had happened to him, the terror still holding him in its grip. There was no sign of the spider crabs, but as they passed the first of the ruins – Charlie's family home – they could hear a rustling sound.

'It's the seaweed, moving in the wind,' said Jenny.

'There isn't any wind.' David gazed around the sands. 'It's dropped.'

'He's dead right.' Terry was shivering violently.

'Don't *use* that word,' hissed Jenny.

'Look at the weed,' muttered David. 'It's got a life of its own.'

The fronds were moving, slowly at first and then with a wet bubbling sound which was dreadful to hear, as if someone was trying to speak with their lungs full of water. Soon the sound became words. *Dance*, harshly rustled the weed voice. *Dance*.

Jenny could hardly believe what was happening. Was this the moment of contact they had been waiting for? All she wanted to do was to race back to the Fisherman's Rest, leap into bed and pull the covers over her head. Then she desperately pulled herself together, knowing that she and David had summoned the Drowned and this was her one chance to communicate with them. Somehow, she forced herself to speak.

'Don't take Charlie. That's what we've come to ask you. Please don't take him.'

He's ready, rasped the weed.

'Rose doesn't want him to come. Rose doesn't like being with you. You shouldn't have taken her.'

She was ready.

'It had nothing to do with her. You're lying. You're just searching for victims. You tried to drown me. You just tried to drown Terry.'

He's been selected.

'No,' wept Terry. 'No!'

'You're evil,' shouted Jenny, losing her temper. 'Completely evil.'

David looked at her in horror. This was the opportunity they'd risked everything for and she had completely blown it.

The roaring sound behind them began so abruptly that they turned away from the rasping whisper of the weed to see the huge wave boiling up from the pit, gathering strength as it thundered towards them, curling dark green and glistening, filled with the swollen faces of the Swinton Drowned. Men, women, old and young, even a boy of about their own age, travelled towards them with furious speed, their features bloated, skin flaccid, bulbous lips and withered eyes all in the wave that rose higher and higher, emitting the smell of rotting plankton.

'Run,' yelled Jenny. 'They're out to get us.'

They pounded over the flat wet sand, but the surface soon petered out into the boggy mud they had waded through before.

The rotting smell thickened and they slowed down hopelessly as the wave broke, dragging them backwards, the pull so strong that it was like sliding down a chute into a swimming pool. The drowned church of Swinton was waiting for them, and David and Jenny knew that it was only a matter of time before the silky shrouds caught hold.

As the wave ripped back over the sand, Jenny

could just make out David's and Terry's heads in the sheet of white foam, while above them the moon turned the sea a jaundiced yellow and the stars gleamed mockingly. The dragging seemed to go on for a very long time, and David knew they were off the shelf and over the church. The Swinton Drowned must have been playing with them, but now the deadly game was over and they were to join Rose and the other victims.

Suddenly the dragging stopped and all three found they were treading water. Despite the darkness the water was incredibly clear, as if it had been lit from beneath, and they could see everything in the minutest detail.

The Drowned were embedded in the weed around St Stephen's, gazing up, their lips parted in soft snarls, their faces enormous. Among them David and Jenny saw a young man surprisingly wearing a top hat, his hair drooping down his cheeks like rats' tails. He was grinning maliciously and Jenny wondered if he could be the lover of Nathaniel's wife.

Around the church with its ruined spire and roofless nave was a graveyard, and from the open tombs rose the shrouds. They began to snake up towards them, while the Drowned clapped their puffy hands together in delight, bubbles coming from their mouths while little silver fish swam through their weed-like hair. Then the bell began to make its hollow booming and, for the first time, Jenny and David could see it swinging between the barnacled rafters.

A woman in a scarf and a print dress drifted up towards them, her face pale and swollen, her body almost translucent. She was elderly, with grey hair.

'Rose!' yelled Terry. 'Rose. You're alive down there. I'll rescue you. I'll get you out.'

She shook her head and waved an admonishing finger at him. Then Rose turned to the shrouds and gestured at them urgently. Her voice came into both the twins' heads. *It's not time yet. They're not ready for the dance.* The shrouds returned to the open tombs and the stone lids firmly shut. The seaweed was streaming away from one of the graves, detaching itself to reveal the headstone on which there was a familiar and ominous inscription: WE'LL TAKE A CHILD FOR THE HARM HE DID.

'Watch out!' yelled David.

The block of wood seemed to hurl itself up from the depths, narrowly avoiding Jenny, floating on the surface with the scratched words: WE'LL TAKE YOU ALL FOR THE HARM YOU DO.

Then they saw that Terry was no longer on the

surface. He was diving down towards Rose.

'Get him!' David kicked and dived, rapidly followed by Jenny. Once they were under water, the twins opened their eyes and saw that the deadly group below had adopted a greeny sheen and were wafting to and fro as if they were weeds at the bottom of the pit. Jenny could see livid white flat fish floundering their way out of the nave of the chapel. The bell was silent. Then the Drowned disappeared, vanishing into the folds of the seaweed. Rose had been right. They were not ready. As yet they still hadn't the strength for the dance. Jenny and David saw Terry shooting towards the surface, his arms and legs cleaving the water, heading for the light of the moon.

They followed him back up to glorious fresh air, gasping in the freezing water, only to find him preparing to dive again.

'She's down there,' he choked. 'I saw Rose. I'll get her. Charlie will be happy and—'

'She drowned.' David hooked his arm round Terry's neck and they struggled desperately while he kept shouting, 'Don't you understand, you idiot. Rose is dead! Rose is drowned. She's not coming back! Not to anyone.'

Terry lashed out in fury, catching David across the face, and then lashed out again. This time the blow was harder. David let him go while Jenny screamed out, 'Look at your wrist, Terry. Just look at it.'

Words were forming on the wet tanned flesh, words that were not cut but somehow raised up on the surface of his skin. WE'LL TAKE THIS CHILD FOR THE HARM YOU DO.

'What harm *did* I do?' Terry gasped as they swam unmolested towards the tideline, dragging themselves out of the icy waves and on to the cold, flat sand.

'Nothing,' said Jenny.

'You wanted to rescue Rose,' contradicted David. 'And you're a descendant.'

'You saw what they wrote – we're all at risk. It's worse than ever.' Terry was deeply despondent.

'They're powerful,' said Jenny. 'Powerful because they're angry. But they're not ready yet, not strong enough until the tide turns. We've got time.'

David staggered to his feet. 'We've got to find some way of talking them out of it, of stopping all this revenge.'

Terry, however, was looking down at his wrist. 'The words have gone. There's nothing left. Isn't that a good sign?'

'I don't think so,' said David grimly. 'It just means they know you got the message.'

'What about the vicar?' Jenny grabbed at a little ray of hope. 'Suppose he gave them a blessing? It would be like a decent burial, wouldn't it?'

'That's too easy,' said David. 'They might want that, but their anger is so strong it's completely out of control and generating such a powerful force.'

'But why now?' wondered Jenny. 'The Drowned have had plenty of opportunity to attack you and your family.'

'What about my great-uncle and aunt and uncle? They got them, didn't they?' yelled Terry. 'They're not doing so bad.'

David ignored him. 'I can't see *why* they suddenly became so *much* stronger.'

'I can,' said Jenny quietly. 'I'm sure it's our fault. I think we've energised them. We've done it in the past, so why not now? Think of all the spirits that have come to us.'

'That was a bit different,' replied David. 'We were able to help them. But the Swinton Drowned aren't asking for help, are they?'

'No,' Jenny admitted.

'I think you're right, though,' said David reluctantly. 'But what can we do about it?' He paused. 'Suppose we go back home to London?'

'They were bad enough before,' muttered Terry. 'When you weren't around. Now they're much more powerful. If that's your fault you can't back out now.'

'We're not.' David was furious.

'There's something else,' said Jenny. 'I think the Drowned might be afraid. Why are they making threats? Trying to kill us? Maybe it was only because Rose intervened that they let us go.'

'Why should Rose influence them? She's just one of their victims. They wouldn't listen to her.' Terry paused and thought. 'Wait a minute. I've got an idea. If we could stop Charlie being taken – or even drowning himself – and if the vicar could bless the waters tonight – isn't there a chance we might weaken them?'

'No,' said Jenny. 'I don't think that's enough. They're really strong. But what about the victims? The innocent people the Drowned took in revenge. Like Rose. Like your relations, Terry. *They* can't want revenge against Nathaniel's descendants. They're more likely to want revenge against the Swinton Drowned!'

'In other words,' said David slowly, 'they might start a mutiny down there. Can't we reach the victims? Get them to be more militant?'

As he spoke a long thin slither of cold water

trickled across the sand, licking icily at his ankle.

'The tide's turned,' yelled Terry. 'They'll be coming for us.'

CHAPTER TWELVE

'What are you lot running from?' Charlie Hamilton was standing waiting for them at the edge of the shingle, having watched Terry, Jenny and David charging across the sands, panting and gasping until they reached the relative safety of the pebble beach.

The old man looked disgruntled and Jenny saw that he was still glancing out to sea, watching the tide gradually creep over the muddy wastes.

'We thought we'd have a race,' she gasped. 'Just to see who could get back first. But it looks as if it's a dead heat.'

David sniggered and she realised she had inadvertently used the word she was coming to detest – 'dead'. Somehow she couldn't get it out of her mind.

'Why are you soaked then?'

'The tide almost caught us.'

There was terror in the old man's eyes.

'You don't want to be around tonight,' he said.

'Not with the dead dancing.'

'I thought you were meant to be working in the bar,' said Terry bluntly.

'Just came out for a breath of air. I'm hoping your dad's not noticed I've gone.' Charlie paused and then added, 'You lock the doors tonight. It's exactly a year since my Rose died, so I hope they dance with me. I'm ready. I want my Rose.'

He's ready. David remembered the weeds rasping Charlie's name. 'Don't you *hate* the Swinton Drowned?'

'I'd rather be amongst them than be here without my Rose.'

'You can't do it, Charlie,' said Terry desperately. 'You can't leave us. Not me and Dad and Mum. You're part of the family. We need you!'

'So does Rose,' the old man replied doggedly.

'Does she?' Jenny was angry now. 'I bet you she doesn't want to see you dead. Terry's right – you're just being selfish. You've no right to be. You're like a grandfather to Terry and a father to Aunty Betty and Uncle Trevor. You can't leave them now!'

Charlie hesitated and Jenny plunged on, watched admiringly by the two boys.

'They love you. They can't be without you. They need protection.'

'Protection?' The old man gazed at her. 'From who?'

'You know who.'

'The dead?'

'Suppose the dead dance with *them*?'

Charlie Hamilton was quiet and David realised that Jenny was making him think. If she won him over, a vital blow against the Swinton Drowned would have been struck.

'Look at Terry. Remember what he's been through this last year, worrying about tonight. Don't make him worse. Can't you promise that you'll stay in your room? No one's safe, including the Todds. You don't understand, do you?' she continued. 'Uncle Trevor's a descendant of Nathaniel's. So is Terry. Are you going to desert them at a time like this?'

'I know all that,' said Charlie shortly. 'But they've never been in trouble before.'

'But the Drowned are more powerful tonight. More powerful than they've ever been.'

'And why would that be?'

She certainly wasn't going to tell him. Jenny knew she could only go so far with Charlie.

Then Terry took over. 'You know the instruments we found – all clogged up like they are. The harmonicas and the accordion?'

'What about them?'

'I think you should burn them.'

'Why?'

'Because if you do it'll show them that you mean business. That you're not prepared to dance. That you mean to defy them.' Jenny and David could see the old man was still wavering, torn between Rose and his 'adopted' family.

'I don't know about defying them.'

'You've got to choose between us,' said Terry miserably. 'I know how much you loved Rose. I loved her too. We all did. But don't you love *us*? How can you leave me and Mum and Dad? I've seen that message, carved in the driftwood. Have *you* seen it, Charlie?'

'What message?'

'WE'LL TAKE A CHILD FOR THE HARM HE DID. Well, like it or not, they'll probably take me. They might even try for Dad, and if you volunteer – that'll leave Mum.'

'Load of tommyrot,' muttered Charlie, looking hangdog and badly shaken. 'But I—'

'Charlie!' Uncle Trevor was standing by the door of the Fisherman's Rest, yelling down to the beach in concern. 'Come back here. Fast as you can. *Please*, Charlie!'

Slowly the old man turned and walked away

without looking back, his feet scrunching over the pebbles.

'Do you think I convinced him?' Terry asked Jenny.

Before she could reply, David said quietly, 'I'm sorry, but I don't think you did. He loves you and your family, Terry. Unfortunately he loved Rose that little bit more.'

'I think David's right,' said Jenny bleakly.

Terry looked devastated.

'How long have we got?' asked David.

'High tide's in the early hours,' said Terry vaguely, trying to recover. 'Do you think Charlie senses you've got powers, that you've made the Swinton Drowned more powerful by mistake?'

'I don't know,' said Jenny. 'I just think he's very torn, that's all.'

'What are we going to do? Lock all the doors of the pub?' Terry was beginning to panic. 'We haven't even come clean with my parents yet, and I don't know if they'd accept any of it if we did.'

'We've got to try,' said David. 'We've got to keep Charlie in – and the Drowned out. Somehow. Do you reckon they can get at us through stone walls?'

'I don't know,' said Jenny. 'Walls haven't exactly stopped ghosts in the past, have they?'

'If we're locked inside the pub,' began David, 'we could be giving the Drowned more strength.'

'Maybe we could turn it against them,' wondered Jenny.

'How?'

'I don't know,' she admitted.

'I'll tell you this.' Terry was adamant. 'I'd rather have you two in the Fisherman's than out. The dead could just turn up and pick us off. At least with you around we're in with a chance.'

Not much of one, thought Jenny. They still had no idea how to contact the drowned victims, how to stir up a mutiny, and they *had* to do something. 'I'm going to the phone box on the harbour,' she said. 'I'm going to call the vicar.'

'You'd better hurry.' Terry was panicking. 'You know the tide's turned.'

'I'm coming with you.' David was immediately protective.

'Terry, you stay and try to get Charlie settled.' Jenny was giving orders now. 'We shan't be long.'

'Why not phone from the pub?'

'We won't convince your parents if they overhear us. They'll think we're crazy – whatever they already half believe.'

*

'Where's the tide?' asked Jenny as they raced along the harbour wall. She could easily have looked for herself, but she didn't want to, didn't dare.

'Creeping up,' was all David would tell her.

'Fast or slow?'

'At its usual pace. We've got time,' he told her encouragingly. David didn't know whether phoning the vicar was going to do any good, but he supposed they had to try everything. Never had he felt so defenceless.

The harbour was deserted, the fishing boats keeled over at an angle, resting on the mud. Only a few people were on the streets but the pubs were full, exuding dim music and once some muted cheering.

The telephone box was alongside the harbour master's office and David squeezed himself in while Jenny got directory enquiries to find the number of the rectory for her. When she dialled, the phone rang for a long time and was eventually answered testily.

'Yes?'

'Reverend Moore?'

'Speaking.' He was making an effort to be more polite now.

'I'm sorry to ring so late. This is Jenny Golding, speaking from a call box at the harbour. You remember you met my brother and me down on the beach the other day.'

'Hurry up,' urged David. He couldn't see the beach from the box, but in his mind the Swinton Drowned were already dancing their way towards them.

'How can I help you?'

'A lot's happened. I can't tell you now. But the Drowned are active tonight. They're after me and my brother and my cousin and Charlie and my Uncle Trevor who's—'

Reverend Moore cut into her breathless explanation irritably. 'Are you playing a joke?'

'Of course not.'

'Then I don't understand—'

'The tide's turned. The Swinton Drowned are coming in to dance with the living.'

'Surely you don't believe such nonsense—'

'It isn't nonsense. They've tried to drown me twice. We're psychic and—'

'Look. This is ridiculous.' The vicar was trying to be a little more soothing now. 'You're getting worked up over superstition. I know some of the adults round here believe in this legend, but I think it's monstrous that they should have been filling your heads with—'

'They haven't,' Jenny insisted. 'We just want you to bless the waters.'

'I can't. Not until the Parochial Church Council agrees. It would have to be put on a new agenda and debated at the next meeting. As you know, it's something I'd like to do, first of all for the dead souls, secondly to allay this absurd superstition. But when I hear all this from the mouths of children I do wonder about Swinton.'

'We want you to bless the waters tonight,' pleaded Jenny hopelessly, knowing that her request was going to come to nothing, knowing that the Drowned were advancing on the tide.

'I've got no permission.'

'You don't need it.'

'Of course I do. Now look here, why don't you go back home and—'

Unable to bear the situation any longer, David prodded his sister in the ribs and hissed at her, 'It's going to be too late. They'll be on the beach soon.'

'So you won't do the blessing tonight?'

'I can't.'

Jenny slammed down the phone.

'Let's go,' yelled David. 'We're running out of time.'

The twins dashed back along the harbour wall, and down on to the shingle beachhead, stumbling and almost falling because their eyes were on the rapidly approaching tide. The sea was covering the sand in great swathes and David was sure he could see lights beyond the ruins. They ran as they had never run before and arrived at the Fisherman's Rest gasping and panting.

It was eleven and already the patrons were starting to leave. The locals went home hurriedly, keeping to the streets, while a few unknowing visitors straggled across the beach towards the hotels on the other side of Swinton.

Terry, meanwhile, had called a meeting in the kitchen and he, David and Jenny sat round the table drinking mugs of cocoa with Charlie Hamilton and their uncle and aunt. The atmosphere was increasingly tense as they all listened to the relentless beating of the waves on the beach.

'We've got to lock all the doors, Dad – and bolt the windows. We shouldn't go to sleep either,' said Terry in considerable agitation.

Betty and Trevor Todd exchanged glances and then looked at Charlie who was subdued and gloomy. Jenny was suddenly aware that an excuse was being made, a cover-up so that the situation could appear to be more rational. The degree of belief the six of them held in the Swinton Drowned was to remain unspoken. Charlie was the immediate problem. They had to stop him trying to commit suicide by walking into the sea.

Jenny and David mutually decided they wouldn't mention their frustrating conversation with the vicar, despite Terry's agonised glances.

Uncle Trevor took it upon himself to assert authority. 'I'm sorry, Charlie,' he began. 'I'm going to lock you in your room tonight.'

'You can't do that.' The old man was immediately aggressive.

'I can and will. You're precious to us and we know how you feel, tonight of all nights. I'm also going to make this place secure and keep the keys to myself. I'm sorry, but it seems to me that this is what I should be doing.'

'You can't take away a man's liberty.'

'Unfortunately I have to. I've got to keep you safe for your own sake until the danger's over. And the reason is we all love you.'

'That's right,' said Betty. 'You've been a father to me — a father to us all. I want to keep you safe tonight and every night.'

Jenny felt close to tears, but Charlie was looking truculent.

'If I want to top myself I can do it any time.'

'You know — we know — what you think about tonight,' said Aunty Betty as tactfully as she could manage. 'We don't think it would be a possibility at any other time and neither do you.' She laid a hand on the old man's arm. 'Please, Charlie. Remember how much we all care for you.'

'OK,' said Uncle Trevor, getting to his feet. 'I'm going to start locking up.'

'I'll help you, Dad,' offered Terry.

'I'll take you up on that, son.' He turned to Charlie again. 'Look how my boy's changed. I'm sure much of that's due to his cousins.' He grinned warmly at the twins. 'So if he can get out of his mood, surely you can do the same, Charlie.'

'I want my Rose,' said the old man sourly. 'I want to go to her.'

'You've got the most wonderful memories of her. Rose would want you to hang on to those.' Aunty Betty also got to her feet. 'She wouldn't want you to drown. You know she wouldn't.'

'How can you be so sure?' said Charlie irritably. 'You can lock me in. I'll be your prisoner,' he added rather childishly.

But for how long? wondered David.

CHAPTER THIRTEEN

Jenny was determined to stay awake, but once she was in bed an insistent drowsiness came over her. David slipped quietly into his sister's room with his duvet. He stretched out on the floor, determined not to give in to sleep. But the breaking waves were like a lullaby, sending the twins into soothing sleep just when they should have been at their most alert.

David woke with a start to find his fingers tapping rhythmically on the floor. He was enjoying the tune, which was familiar although he couldn't work out what it was. A pop song? No. Something he had heard on the TV? Or at school? The shock when he remembered was as intense as if someone had punched him hard in the stomach. The reedy voices outside bubbled and the words were hard to make out. But they were getting clearer – and closer.

David leapt up, shaking Jenny awake.

'Get up!' he said. 'They're here.'

She sat up at once and gave a shiver.

'They're here,' repeated David. 'And they're stronger than ever. Can't you feel them?'

They ran to the window and swept the curtains aside. It was midnight – and time for the dance.

The Swinton Drowned were rising from the sea in a phosphorescent glow. There must have been at least a hundred of them, dressed in mouldering finery, swaying to the rhythm, their swollen lips parted in delight, their watery eyes huge and unblinkingly wide open.

The tide was in, the sand had gone and the water was lapping at the pebbles.

The young man in the top hat led the straggling line while the musicians rose from the waves with drum and flute, accordion and harmonica, the sound bubbling until the salt water drained from the instruments. The young man danced and swayed and then seemed to float towards an upturned rowing boat on which were laid a number of objects that glowed in the moonlight.

He rubbed his wet hands together and beckoned on the ghostly procession.

'I know what those are,' muttered David. 'Charlie must have slipped back and put them there last night before Uncle Trevor locked him in.'

'The harmonicas and the accordion,' breathed Jenny.

The Swinton Drowned were circling the boat in their dozens, and as the young man held the instruments aloft a ragged cheer went up and their translucent bodies seemed to harden, to grow in strength and purpose.

The young man began to scratch with his nail on the side of the old boat and then he looked up at the twins with a smile that was deadly in its menace. The Drowned moved aside and David and Jenny knew that they didn't want to mask the message that they were sure was meant for them.

WE'LL TAKE YOU FOR THE HARM YOU DO.

Slowly, but with precision, the Swinton Drowned spread out, gripping each other's damp and distorted hands and forming a circle, dancing around the upturned boat and singing in bubbling voices.

'*Will you dance with the dead, my merry little friends?*
Will you dance? Will you dance?
Till your lives do end?
Will you dance with the dead, my merry little friends?
Will you sing? Will you shout?
Until the Drowned come all about?'

Already David was beating out the rhythm on

the windowsill and Jenny was tapping her feet and humming to the song.

'We've got to stop,' he yelled but they couldn't resist the tune.

David pulled the curtain across and the song and its accompaniment became more muffled. Exerting tremendous willpower he found he was able to control his hands.

'It's the rhythm,' Jenny panted.

'It's deadly,' he replied fearfully. Then he peered out of the window again and grabbed Jenny's arm in rising excitement. 'Wait a minute!'

'What is it?'

'Can't you see?'

Not all the Swinton Drowned were dancing; a small group of onlookers stood by the waves on the tideline, watching mournfully.

'Who are they?'

'The victims. They *must* be! Those who have danced with the dead – victims of the Swinton Drowned. They're not joining in the dance. *They* don't agree with all this. I'm sure of that.'

'But how can they help us?' asked Jenny.

'I don't know.' David gazed down at the group thoughtfully.

There were about twenty of them, all with white, swollen faces but with a shimmering, shifting shape to their bodies. An elderly woman in a scarf had slightly detached herself from the group and was drifting across the shingle and gazing up at the pub.

'Is that Rose?' asked Jenny.

'I think so.' David was hesitant. 'We daren't go out there. They know who we are.'

'They're not getting us,' said Jenny firmly, pulling the curtains across tightly. 'We've only got to stick it out until the tide turns. Then they'll have to go back and the dance will be over.'

Then, without warning, the bedroom door was flung open.

Terry dashed to the window and wrenched it open before David or Jenny could stop him.

'Don't *do* that, you raving idiot,' yelled David.

But he was too late.

The rhythm filled the room, and Terry's feet began to tap and his body began to sway. Fighting to prevent himself from joining in, David pushed Terry aside, closed the window and drew the curtains again, despite the fact that his hands were beating time to the music while Jenny behind him was swaying to the terrible song.

As soon as it was muffled the need to dance to the rhythm faded, but within seconds the music seemed to get slightly louder, as if the Drowned had found even greater strength, as if they were moving towards the peak of their powers.

'Is the tide full?' Jenny yelled at Terry.

'Almost,' he muttered.

'Any minute now we'll be forced out on to the beach, unlocking doors as we go,' said David.

'I was a fool to open the window,' said Terry, looking ashamed.

David shook his head. 'They're out to get all of us. Don't make a mistake like that again.'

'I'm sorry,' Terry repeated. 'I've checked Charlie. Dad's done a good job by locking him in on the top floor and taking away the key. I could hear him prowling up and down in there so I reckon he's safe.'

'Can he open the window?' demanded Jenny.

'Dad bolted it. Charlie moaned away but we didn't give in. There's only one thing' – Terry paused uncertainly – 'I can't wake my parents. I've tried, but – I can't. They seem so deeply asleep.'

David and Jenny remembered how they had tried to fight sleep and failed. Was this another trick? Did the Swinton Drowned want to catch them all unawares?

'You gave them more strength,' snapped Terry. 'Remember?'

'You're right,' replied David unhappily. 'But

we're a threat to them too. They've made that pretty clear. WE'LL TAKE YOU FOR THE HARM YOU DO,' he repeated miserably. 'OK, we *can* accidentally make them more powerful by just being around, but they also know we're out to stop them taking the living.'

'So how *are* we going to stop them?' stuttered Terry, even more unnerved.

'The only thing we can do is rely on the goodness of the people they snatched,' replied Jenny. 'But we've got to wait here until the tide turns.'

As she spoke the music suddenly came to an abrupt halt. The silence was dreadful.

Then David said, 'We need to know what's happening. I'm going to look outside.'

'No!' yelled Terry. 'You can't do that. You told me not to.'

'We've got to be one up on them.' Jenny was insistent. 'David, go ahead and open the curtains.'

'One up on the Drowned?' laughed Terry hysterically. 'You'll be lucky.'

David quickly drew aside the curtains, but didn't open the window. He gave a whimper of fear.

The Drowned had formed two columns and were holding flabby hands, moving towards the Fisherman's Rest, their swollen faces upraised and their eyes focused malignantly on the bedroom window.

'I'm going to try and wake Dad and Mum again,' yelled Terry and dashed out of the room. 'They'll be trapped. Trapped in sleep when the Drowned arrive.'

'They're not arriving anywhere,' Jenny shouted at him. 'All the doors are locked.' But she was hardly thinking what she was saying.

'That won't keep them out. You know that,' muttered David. 'It's hopeless, isn't it? Why should spirits be put off by bolts and locks? We must have been mad to think they would be.'

Jenny knew he was right. But still the music hadn't started again and nor had the song. Was that a sign of hope?

Then they heard an immense crashing and thumping and banging, followed by the splintering of wood. Charlie was breaking down the door of his room upstairs.

'Why's he being so selfish?' David was scornful.

Charlie appeared at the head of the second flight of stairs. 'Don't try and stop me,' he said quietly. His eyes seemed glazed, as if he didn't recognise them.

'How can we?' Jenny said. 'But I know Rose doesn't want you.'

'How do *you* know?' The old man seemed to

lose confidence for a moment.

'Because we've talked to them.' David made it sound the most natural state in the world.

'To the Swinton Drowned?' Charlie gazed at them in astonishment.

'Rose was on the beach last night. And she's outside now.'

The old man gazed at him in amazement.

'Why didn't you tell me?'

'Because we knew that you'd go to her,' said Jenny.

'She won't be lonely if I join her.'

'Don't you understand?' David yelled at the old man. 'She's a victim, like the others.'

Charlie hesitated. 'I want to be with my Rose,' he insisted. 'So get out of the way.'

'No,' said David. 'I won't let you go.'

Terry came pounding down the corridor, his eyes wide with panic. 'I still can't wake Mum and Dad. I've tried shaking them, but it's no good. I need help.'

'So does Charlie,' David warned him. 'We've got to keep him inside.'

Terry looked up at the old man. 'How did you get out?'

'Broke down the door, didn't I?'

'Dad will be furious.'

116

'I don't care. I'll soon be with my Rose. You see if I'm not.'

'We're not letting you go out there.' Terry squared up to him. 'Are we, David?'

'No chance.'

'You're not to hurt Charlie.' Jenny was suddenly afraid. 'This isn't the time for a fight.'

'I'll take you two boys apart,' said Charlie.

'Come on then!' Terry replied belligerently.

Charlie Hamilton hurled himself down the narrow staircase, eyes full of rage, his fists clenched.

The so-called fight was over in seconds. Charlie simply tapped Terry on the chest, sending him flying on to the landing floor, and when David rushed into the fray Charlie pushed him away so hard that he, too, went down and rolled into Terry.

'Right.' The old man rubbed his hands together and grinned. 'Sorry about that, miss. But they were in the way and I didn't hurt them.'

He then shambled stiffly down the stairs and she heard him bashing away at the back door until it gave way, with a rending of wood and smashing of glass.

'Are you two OK?' asked Jenny anxiously.

David was the first to pick himself up.

'You shouldn't have taken him on. An old man like that.'

'Thanks for the sympathy.'

Terry took longer to get to his feet, coughing and spluttering. 'We've got to get him back.'

'Go out among the Drowned?' David gazed at him as if he was crazy.

'They'll take a child for the harm you do,' Jenny quoted.

'That's a risk we've got to take,' shouted Terry as he made for the stairs. Before either of the twins could stop him, he was charging towards the back door.

'We'll have to go too,' said Jenny.

'This could be the last decision we ever take,' protested David.

But Jenny was already heading after Terry.

The beach was deserted and the Swinton Drowned had disappeared. The high tide was lapping at the pebbles and there was an ominous stillness in the air, as if something was waiting to pounce.

'I don't believe this,' said David. 'It *must* be a trap.'

'There they are.'

The old man was leaning against the breakwater, his head bowed, while Terry talked to him gently.

'I think Charlie's crying,' said Jenny miserably.

'OK,' snapped David. 'Let's try and get them

both back inside.' Then he saw that the back door was swinging off its hinges. 'Not exactly secure this place, is it?'

'You can't keep ghosts out,' Jenny told him. 'You told *me* that. Let's go and see what we can do.'

They checked the beach and the sea as they scrunched across the pebbles, but there was no sign of the Swinton Drowned or their victims. When they reached Terry, the old man was sobbing bitterly.

'He saw Rose. She was standing on the beach waiting for him. She told Charlie to go back inside, and if he tried to kill himself she'd never speak to him again.'

'Not much chance of that,' observed David, but Terry was too upset to understand.

'Did she say anything else?' asked Jenny.

'She said she loved me.' Charlie made a desperate attempt to control his shaking voice. 'And that if she could have a decent Christian burial we'd both meet in heaven. When my life was run.'

'Isn't that just what *should* happen?'

'I could live for years.'

'You might,' said David bluntly. 'But maybe not if the Swinton Drowned are still hanging about. I don't understand what they're up to. The tide's high. They should be at the height of their powers. So where are they?'

'They're not here,' said Jenny. 'And if they were going to take Charlie, surely they would have done so by now. After all, he *is* on their hit list. Like us. Like your dad, Terry. Like you!'

'She said they didn't want me,' whispered Charlie. 'The Drowned were looking for other victims.'

'Which victims?' David was getting very worked up now.

'They must have rejected Charlie on Rose's instructions. I didn't think they ever listened to their victims.' Jenny was puzzled. 'Maybe I was right and they're not *all* evil.' She began to look more hopeful. 'Do you think there *could* be a mutiny? If so, we've got a chance.'

As she spoke, the hollow booming of the bell began yet again.

'If there *is* a chance of mutiny,' said David, 'it's us who've got to organise it.'

For the moment they decided to make a tactical withdrawal while a plan was made.

Once they were back in the pub, Charlie began to check the windows and try to repair the broken door, while Terry, Jenny and David ran up the stairs to the bedroom where Betty and Trevor

Todd were still sleeping so deeply.

Terry gazed down at his parents hopelessly, while Jenny and David shook them, gently at first and then more vigorously. But they were unwakeable.

Suddenly the deadly rhythm filled the room once more. David, Jenny and Terry used all their willpower to shut it out, but already they could hear Charlie singing downstairs in a cracked growl.

'Will you dance with the dead . . .'

Covering their ears, they blocked out the dreadful sound, but within seconds the music was in their heads.

Charlie was bellowing the first line of the song again. 'Will you dance with the dead, my merry little friends?' It was like a personal challenge from the Swinton Drowned as their music became ever louder.

Jenny yelled at David and Terry, their ears still covered, 'It's no good. We'll have to go outside. We'll have to organise that mutiny!'

Her twin slowly drew his hands away from his ears. 'Have we got a chance?'

Jenny shook her head. 'I don't know. But we've got to try.'

'Every time we go out there they get stronger. They're feeding off us.'

'We can't go on to the beach.' Terry was horrified. 'They're waiting for me out there. They'll take me into the sea.'

'If we stay here, they'll come for us.' With her hands beating time to the music Jenny ran down the stairs, while David and Terry, their heads swimming with the rhythm, followed.

CHAPTER FOURTEEN

When David and Jenny arrived back on the beach, they saw the Drowned had returned from the sea and were dancing in a slow-moving circle, linking flabby, swollen hands with Terry and Charlie. As the rhythm increased, the circle began to move faster, barely making contact with the ground. In the bright moonlight there must have been a hundred phantoms and four frail humans. To the wail of the harmonica and the accordion the dead danced with the living.

David noticed that the circle was gradually moving nearer to the edge of the sea, to the little lapping wavelets that looked so innocent but were growing bigger as a scudding breeze sprang up. Then, above the sound of the instruments, David could once again hear the hollow chiming of St Stephen's bell.

The Swinton Drowned were a forbidding sight. Spectres of men, women and children of all ages, with bloated faces and sunken eyes, that gazed ahead until they alighted on David and Jenny. Then they grinned, stretching their flaccid lips, their bubbling smiles exposing green teeth while seaweed clung to their hair and protruded from their ears.

The musicians stood in the centre of the circle, the dark melody once more gaining in speed.

Jenny and David tried desperately to stop their feet tapping and their hands clapping, but the all-embracing rhythm was irresistible. If they could only stop themselves being drawn into the circle! Then, with a cry of terror, Jenny ran forward and the circle opened for her as she swayed towards the whirling shapes of the Swinton Drowned.

To David's horror, he saw his sister dancing with the dead as the circle gathered speed.

David threw himself at it, grabbing at the spectral hands that held Jenny so tightly. He touched a soft pulpy mass and fell back with a cry of disgust. Trying again, he wrenched at the stuff, but this time he got through the soggy flesh to feel tendons below: but now they were tubers of weed, knotted, slippery. The Swinton Drowned had become part of the depths that had claimed them.

Jenny was held fast by the young man in the top hat on one side, and on the other by an elderly woman in a headscarf. David was gasping for breath, dancing fast to keep up with the whirling circle, and as he did so he could just make out a woman's voice whispering against the strident sound of the band.

As the whispering began to penetrate his mind – *Will you dance with the dead, my merry little friend? Will you dance? Will you dance? Till your life does end?* – in the middle of the verse, came other words, furtively inserted, as if an opportunity had been seized. *Join the circle if you want to save her. Join the circle if you want to save her.*

'You're trapping me!' yelled David.

NO! Rose's voice seemed to thunder in his head like the tide. *We were taken against our will. But there are enough of us now. We won't allow any more.*

'How can you be so sure?'

We'll break the dance. You'll see. You must give us your strength.

'How?'

Believe in us. Believe in our strength to resist them.

Suddenly the young man leant back towards David, his swollen features twisted in a grin. David felt the soft grip of damp tendons, but the weed held strong.

Jenny's hand, warm and firm, slipped into his own and David was off into the whirling dance. His feet didn't seem to touch the pebbles at all, and

125

his nostrils were filled with the smell of rotting weed.

Fight them, came Rose's voice in his head. David tried to resist; the circle grew smaller, the drowned eyes brighter, as they all headed towards the cold, dark sea. The hollow booming was louder, the musicians dimmer. Panic surged in David's chest. 'Stop!' he yelled. 'You've got to stop. You can't take us with you. Not into the sea.'

But all he could hear was bubbling laughter and the crashing of the cruel waves on the shingle.

David felt Jenny's hand slacken. Had Rose let her go? And what about the others? Then he felt the cold and weedy grip of the young man in the top hat tighten on his wrist.

Let them go. Let them go, said Rose's voice in his head, but David knew she was wrong; there were too few victims and the Swinton Drowned had overruled them. Soon the clamour became even greater as a great bubbling shout went up from the Drowned. *We'll take them all for the harm he did.*

The circle was turning in the shallows now and David could feel the numbing cold of the dark and glistening sea.

Suddenly the circle seemed to hesitate, to slow down, and he heard Rose's voice in his head talking to the Drowned. *Let them go. Let's just let them go.*

There were the lights under the sea again and a bubbling sound offshore was followed by a roaring. For a moment David wondered if another tidal wave was coming, but out to sea the water seemed calm. It was the sea bed that was erupting.

The surface seemed to boil and then David saw the great weed-hung husk of the ruined church with its broken spire, its bell ringing, muffled no longer, rising from the depths. The gaping windows were lit by a greenish light, the walls glowed with barnacles like rubies and fish poured from what once had been the porch.

The sound of mocking, bubbling laughter filled his ears and David found himself being swept head-first into the icy waves.

When he surfaced, St Stephen's had disappeared again and so had the Drowned, but already a strong current was pulling him out to sea. David had never experienced such an undertow before, and the more he swam against it the faster it seemed to take him.

Jenny passed him, lying on her back, her face twisted in terror. He tried to make a grab at her and failed.

'They were too strong,' she choked. 'Rose and the others didn't stand a chance.'

'They've only taken the victims they wanted,' spluttered David who had just glanced back at the beach. 'Like us and Terry.'

Charlie stood on the shingle, gazing out to sea. David saw him dash into the waves to try to help them, but the sea was too rough, too strong. He tried again and again but the sea was determined to keep him out. Eventually the old man lay gasping on the pebbles while the waves roared like lions.

CHAPTER FIFTEEN

When the silky stuff gripped her round the ankles Jenny gave a scream of terror, remembering the first time the shroud had taken her, knowing that her struggles would only make it tighten even more. Even so, she instinctively kicked out as she was pulled under. There was nothing she could do to release herself and, a few metres away, she saw David and Terry also struggling, and being dragged slowly and relentlessly down.

We'll take a child. The deadly phrase repeated itself over and over again in her mind, and as it did Jenny realised how little any of them could do. The Drowned were vengeful, wanting to punish and go on punishing the living for what Nathaniel Todd had done. The mutiny had not happened – or if it had the rebellion had been swiftly repressed.

As Jenny went under, she desperately held her breath. Opening her eyes again she saw the shrouds around her feet as well as David's and Terry's. They were all being pulled down in the same direction.

The great hulk of the church loomed up in front of them, the weed waving in the nave, the Drowned standing in the rotting pews, silently clapping their sodden hands together in demonic appreciation. Jenny saw a girl of her own age in a mouldering gown waving a skipping rope, pleased to have found a playmate at last.

There's nothing we can do, she thought despairingly. Her lungs were beginning to hurt badly. They could only last a few more seconds.

The hollow booming of St Stephen's drowned bell seemed to completely fill David's head. Then, just as he thought he was going to lose consciousness, he too saw the girl, standing with what he thought might be her parents. She was holding a skipping rope and staring eagerly up at Jenny, who was floating parallel to him now.

David knew he had to reach the girl somehow. He *had* to get her on his side.

You've got your parents, he thought desperately, bellowing the words in his mind, using his willpower so hard that he hurt. *Help us get back to ours.*

As he concentrated, David was conscious that Jenny was doing the same, communicating with the girl, trying to get her on their side.

The girl looked disappointed. She shook her head and David was now sure he was going to drown. His chest seemed to be full of hammer blows, his lungs about to explode. Then the girl looked up at her parents and their watery eyes appeared to soften.

David saw them turn to the ranks of the Drowned and in his head heard the words *Spare them. We must spare them.*

They were in Jenny's mind too, but she also heard other, more hostile statements. *They were selected. They must be taken.*

She was sure she couldn't hold out any longer, she knew the Drowned were indecisive, turning to each other in spectral debate. Her mind was full of their voices as they argued in their bubbling way. *Spare them, spare them,* came one distorted chorus, but the others chanted, *Take them. We must take them.* Then Jenny and David heard Rose's voice in their heads, much clearer than the hissing of the rival factions of the Drowned. *We must let them go. It's not their fault they have psychic strength. They had to stand up against the wickedness.*

Spare then, spare them. The bubbling words grew to a deafening chant which suddenly came to an abrupt halt, followed by a long silence. Then David saw the little girl looking up at her parents pleadingly. The spectral figures nodded, and the shrouds were unwound.

Their limbs released, the twins shot to the surface, drinking in the wonderful life-giving air, ecstatic with relief and the knowledge that Jenny had been right and the Swinton Drowned weren't all evil. They could show mercy. Even love. For a blissful moment David and Jenny trod water, so glad to be alive that they could hardly believe they were. Then they both remembered Terry.

Selfishly they had fought for their own lives but had hardly given their cousin a thought. Of course the Drowned would take him. He was a descendant.

They dived back simultaneously, plunging once more into the abyss until they saw again the roofless church. But there was no sign of the Drowned. Nor was there any sign of Terry.

They've taken him, thought David, and we did nothing to help him. Nothing at all. He had never felt so wretchedly selfish in his life. Despite the fact that his lungs had been ready to burst, he should have fought for Terry's life too.

Still they peered into the green depths, swimming around the weed-hung ruin of a spire, desperately searching. But Terry was nowhere to be seen.

When they both knew they could stay down no

longer, David and Jenny began to cleave their way up to the surface again.

At first they could see only dark swell without any sign of human life. Then they caught sight of their cousin floating on his back in the trough of a wave, gazing up at the stars, looking completely relaxed. After all their efforts, the twins were furious.

'Where have you been?' yelled David, splashing his way over to Terry.

'Yes,' gasped Jenny, enraged. 'Just what do you think you're doing?'

'I came up behind the buoy,' said Terry calmly. 'I saw you diving down again but it was too late. I didn't have the strength to go after you. Anyway, I knew you'd bob up again pretty soon when you couldn't find me.'

'We *did* bob up.' David sounded threatening. 'But we thought the Swinton Drowned had got you.'

'They released me. Like they released you.'

'Let's get back to the shore before they change their minds.' Jenny was shivering violently, although the sea seemed much warmer now the dance was over. 'After all, you *are* a descendant. They spared us and now they're sparing you. That's quite something.'

'It certainly is.' David was still angry, but more out of shock than anything else. 'You'd better get going.'

Terry nodded. Gazing round him fearfully, he turned over on his stomach and began a powerful crawl back to the beach. David and Jenny followed, their arms and legs stiff and sore. Never had they felt so exhausted or relieved.

As Terry struggled out on to the shingle with the twins close behind, they saw a figure watching them intently. For a while, none of them could identify it. Could it be one of the Swinton Drowned? Did the figure have a message to pass on, or, worse still, another threat to give? But as they came closer they realised to their relief that it was the Reverend Moore.

'What's going on?' he asked the shivering trio. 'I couldn't sleep, I kept hearing the bell.' He paused. 'And I kept remembering our conversation.' He looked puzzled and afraid and guilty all at the same time.

Jenny began to explain what had happened. When she had finished the Reverend Moore nodded, and she guessed that he had come to terms with the truth about the Swinton Drowned at last.

'I need to bless the waters. I must do it now – whatever they all say.'

David glanced at Jenny and saw that she knew the blessing wouldn't be enough; they had to convince the Swinton Drowned themselves not to take any more victims.

They were interrupted by the chugging of a motorboat, and above the sound of the engine came a great shout of joy. Seated inside were Uncle Trevor, Aunty Betty and Charlie.

'We thought you'd all drowned,' yelled Trevor, jumping out as the boat nosed into the shallows and throwing his arms around Terry and then David and Jenny. 'Charlie woke us up and told us what had happened. I don't know *why* we slept so heavily.'

Aunty Betty clambered out and embraced them as well. 'We went to get the boat. I was sure we'd be too late, but now it's like a miracle.' She began to cry, hugging Jenny so tightly that it hurt.

'Wait a minute.' Terry bent down and picked up some barnacle-encrusted objects from a bank of shingle. 'The instruments. We'd better get rid of these. Shouldn't we burn them or something?'

'No,' said Charlie, tying the towline of the motorboat to a breakwater and picking up one of the harmonicas. He brought back his arm and hurled it out to sea with an amazingly powerful action. 'Used to be a cricketer,' he explained. 'I can still bowl. Let 'em have the instruments back, I say. They don't belong here.'

David and Jenny and Terry picked up the others and began to throw them out to sea.

The night was still and the wind had died away. Jenny wondered if the Drowned in some way controlled the weather and tide, or were they now just part of the elements?

She stood by the tideline and David joined her. They focused all their attention on the dark waves. *Don't take any more,* Jenny thought, and David used all his willpower to remind the Swinton Drowned. *It's got to be over. You've had your revenge.*

For a while nothing happened; then, just as the Reverend Moore was about to pronounce his blessing, a coffin lid burst out from underneath the sluggish sea, floating into the shallows, the carved message already fading fast. David and Jenny knew it was for their eyes only and caught just a glimpse of the wording. ROSE WANTS AN END. SHE SHALL HAVE HER WISH. THE TAKING IS OVER.

Almost immediately the coffin lid was swept out to sea and the vicar muttered, 'That's odd. I thought I saw—' Then he began to pray, kneeling down and making the sign of the cross as he blessed the waters while the others joined him on the hard shingle. As the Reverend Moore looked out to sea, he said, 'You will do no more harm; neither will you take any more lives. The waters have been blessed and you are released.' He paused and then added, 'A great wrong was done you, but now the dance is over. You are to rest in peace. Amen.'

He stood up, and as Jenny and David scrambled to their feet they heard the drowned bell of St Stephen's begin to toll mournfully. From under the sea there came a great sigh.

'What's that?' whispered Jenny fearfully.

Etched in sharp relief in the moonlight, an object began to float towards them on the waves.

Had the Drowned deceived them and were they about to launch the next round in their campaign of vengeance?

The floppy, squashed-looking object floated through the shallows, and as it came nearer Jenny could see the thing was covered in dark green weed. It was the young man's top hat, and as she watched it turn and tumble in the surf Jenny's fear and anxiety returned. The Drowned were not at rest after all.

'Whatever's that?' asked the vicar uneasily.

'Let's hope it's just a souvenir,' replied Terry nervously.

Charlie walked slowly towards the tideline and Jenny and David followed him. He waded into the shallows and pulled out the sodden and weed-hung hat which was also encrusted with barnacles. When he shook it no ominous message from the Drowned appeared. Then something small and round and gleaming fell out on to the beach. Charlie scrabbled for it on the pebbles. 'I'd know that anywhere. That's my Rose's ring, that is.' He held it up in a shaking hand. 'It's a sign.'

'That she loves you,' said Jenny gently.

'More than that.' Charlie put the ring on his own middle finger. 'Funny,' he muttered. 'That should never fit, but it does. Anyway – it's more than a sign of love.' He sounded confident. 'It means the Swinton Drowned are at rest.'

There was another sigh and a moonlit ripple spread from the abyss where the drowned church lay. 'Do you think they're any happier?' asked David.

'My Rose will be,' said Charlie firmly. 'Now she knows I've come to my senses.'

They all stood in the shallows, gazing out to sea intently, but there were no lights now, only the stars reflected in the dark water.

CHAPTER SIXTEEN

Next day, they were all so exhausted that they slept late. After breakfast, however, Terry suggested taking *Sunrise* out. 'It's a bit like that business of falling off a horse. You've got to get back on fast or you'll never get back on at all. Know what I mean?'

David gave Jenny a faint grin. What a lot had happened in two days.

'I've heard that somewhere before,' Jenny said. 'But maybe we should do a test run and make sure the Drowned aren't – active any longer.' Jenny faltered over the words, but they all three knew they *had* to find out.

Soon *Sunrise* was running before a light breeze and Terry had the spinnaker out, skilfully filling it with what wind there was while Jenny helmed and David and Terry crewed. The sun was a fierce red ball in a cloudless sky, and stowed away in the locker under the stern of the dinghy was one of Aunty Betty's generous picnics.

'You're sure it's a good idea to sail over St Stephen's?' asked Terry.

'You know it is.' David sounded full of purpose. 'OK by you, Jenny?'

She nodded doubtfully.

But when they gazed down into the water as *Sunrise* passed the red buoy the surface was too cloudy to make out anything at all. A sense of anticlimax filled them as Jenny took the dinghy about and sailed back again to St Stephen's.

The breeze had dropped and *Sunrise* was almost stationary, her sails flapping, the three of them apprehensive, waiting, wanting to leave this dreadful spot but still needing to test not just their nerve but the Drowned's intentions.

A bubbling sound came from the depths.

'Let's go,' yelled Terry. 'Come on – what are you waiting for? We don't want it to start up all over again.'

Jenny glanced at David.

'We need to find out what's happening.' David paused and looked back at Swinton. 'For everyone's sake,' he muttered.

The bubbling continued, the sound increasing in volume.

'Something's coming up,' muttered Jenny.

'It'll be another coffin lid,' yelled Terry. 'We've

got to—'

Suddenly dozens of gulls broke surface, miraculously flapping their way from under the surface, their wings flashing a watery sparkle.

Jenny watched them climb higher until they disappeared into the deep blue of the summer sky.

David gazed down at the cloudy sea. 'They've gone,' he whispered. 'The Drowned have released their victims at last.'